Raintree is an imprint of Capstone Global Library Limited, a company incorporated in England and Wales having its registered office at 7 Pilgrim Street, London, EC4V 6LB – Registered company number: 6695582

www.raintree.co.uk
myorders@raintree.co.uk

Editorial project by Atlantyca Dreamfarm S.r.l.

Text by Elisa Puricelli Guerra
Illustrations by Gabo León Bernstein
Translation by Marco Zeni
Original edition published by Edizioni Piemme S.p.A., Italy
Original title: La notte delle tartarughe azzure

British Library Cataloguing in Publication Data
A full catalogue record for this book is available from the British Library.

ISBN 978 1 4747 0440 3
19 18 17 16 15
10 9 8 7 6 5 4 3 2 1

Designer: Rick Korab

Printed and bound in China.

THE NIGHT OF THE BLUE TURTLES

Written by Elisa Puricelli Guerra

Illustrated by Gabo León Bernstein

Contents

WHAT'S HAPPENED SO FAR 8

CHAPTER 1
A SHAMEFUL SHIPWRECK.. 11

CHAPTER 2
THE MYSTERIOUS CABIN BOY 25

CHAPTER 3
TURTLE ISLAND 39

CHAPTER 4
A GOLDEN OMELETTE 57

CHAPTER 5
SEA DOGS 69

CHAPTER 6
FREE REPUBLIC OF THE TURTLES.. 77

CHAPTER 7
LET'S BOARD!.. 97

CHAPTER 8
SCARFACE COLEMAN 111

CHAPTER 9
THE HIDDEN TREASURE.. 123

CHAPTER 10
GENGHIS KHAN IN CORNWALL 137

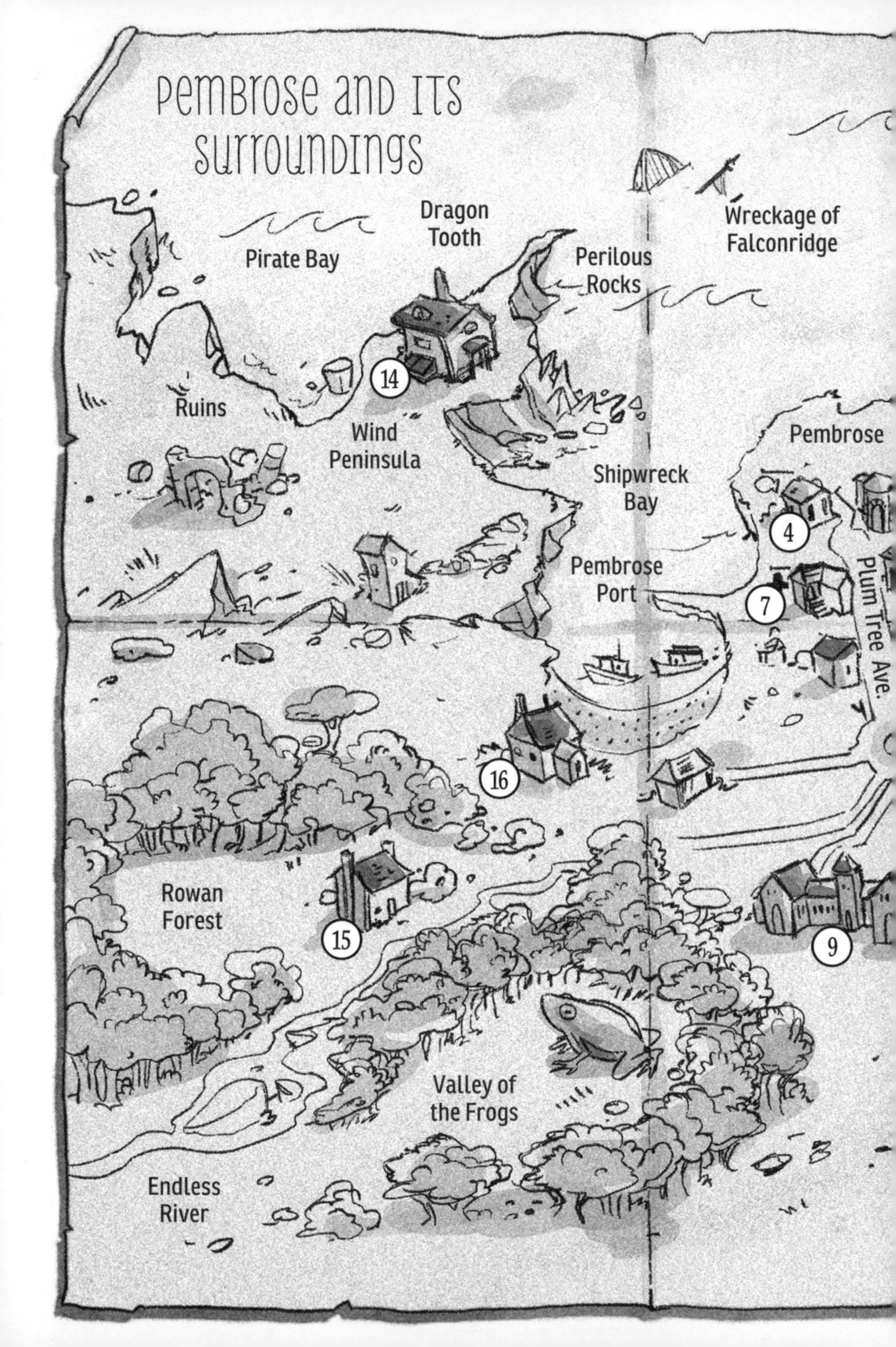
Pembrose and its surroundings
Dragon Tooth
Pirate Bay
Perilous Rocks
Wreckage of Falconridge
14
Ruins
Wind Peninsula
Pembrose
Shipwreck Bay
4
Pembrose Port
7
Plum Tree Ave.
16
Rowan Forest
15
9
Valley of the Frogs
Endless River

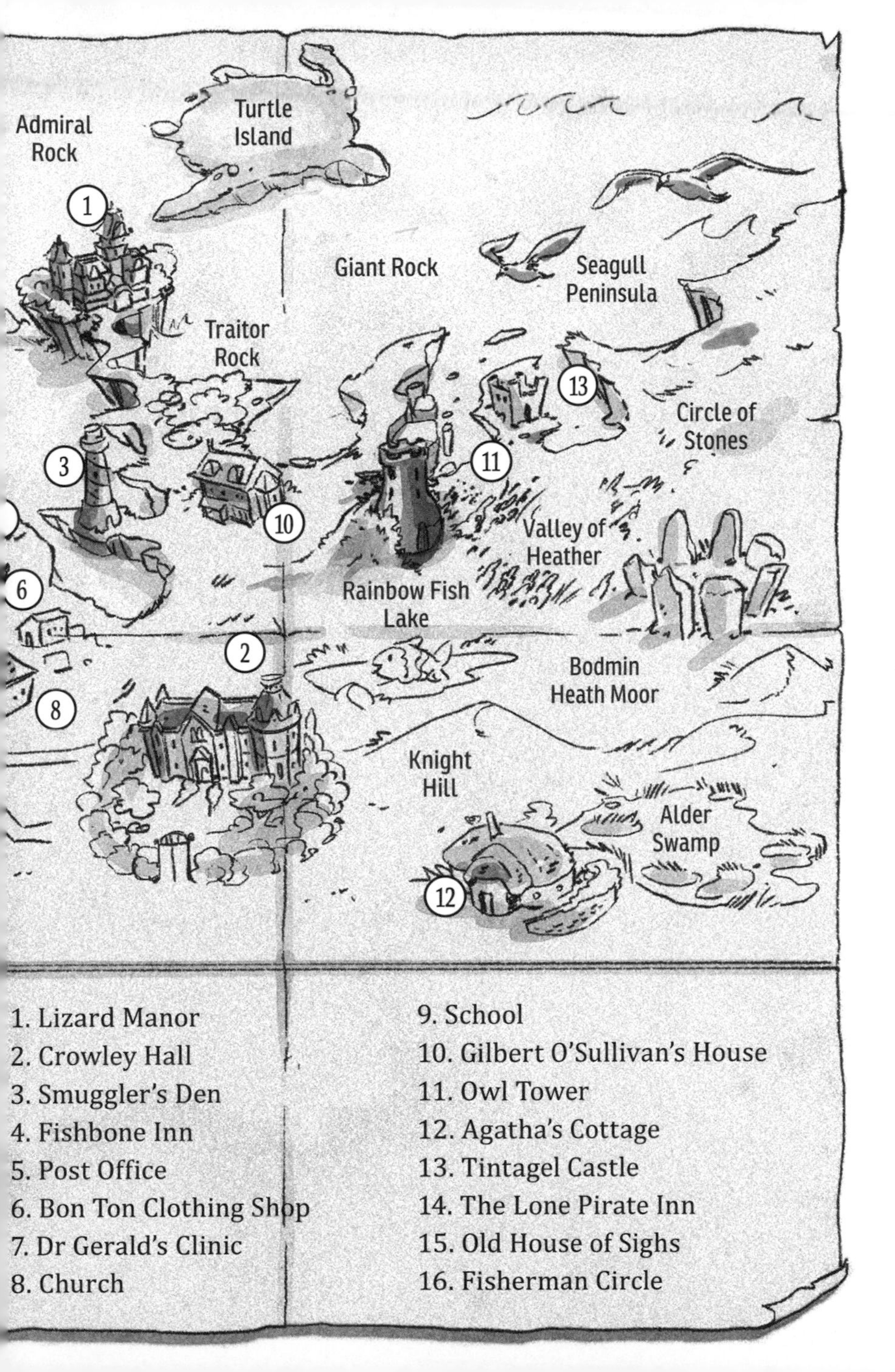
Turtle Island
Admiral Rock
Giant Rock
Seagull Peninsula
Traitor Rock
Circle of Stones
Valley of Heather
Rainbow Fish Lake
Bodmin Heath Moor
Knight Hill
Alder Swamp
1. Lizard Manor
2. Crowley Hall
3. Smuggler's Den
4. Fishbone Inn
5. Post Office
6. Bon Ton Clothing Shop
7. Dr Gerald's Clinic
8. Church
9. School
10. Gilbert O'Sullivan's House
11. Owl Tower
12. Agatha's Cottage
13. Tintagel Castle
14. The Lone Pirate Inn
15. Old House of Sighs
16. Fisherman Circle

WHAT'S HAPPENED SO FAR...

Minerva Mint is a nine-year-old girl who lives in Lizard Manor, a rundown mansion atop Admiral Rock, in Cornwall, England, with fourteen snowy owls, six foxes and a badger called Hugo. She shares the house with Geraldine Flopps, an energetic custodian who found her in a suitcase at Victoria station in London when Minerva was just a baby.

Minerva is determined to find out what happened to her parents, but it is not an easy task. Very few hints were left in the bag with her: a volume from the Universal Encyclopedia, *an envelope addressed to someone called Septimus Hodge, and the deed to the mansion in Cornwall. For nine years she has tried to solve the mystery by herself, but now she finally has help: her new friends Ravi and Thomasina.*

Together, they have found a mysterious little box hidden in a kitchen wall in Lizard Manor. The box contains a small flute whose music can recall hundreds of owls. The top of the box lid is engraved with a picture of a bell-shaped tower and the words Ordo Noctuae, which translates to "Order of the Owls". That's where the friends got the idea for the name of their secret club.

The Order of the Owls even has a headquarters, a tower identical to the one depicted on the little box. Their mission is to unravel the mystery of Minerva's origins. They have already discovered a thing or two: she descends from a pirate and a witch, the beautiful Althea who, before dying almost three hundred years ago, managed to hide a vast treasure. Althea left behind just one hint to find the treasure, passing it on to her newborn baby girl. The children know nothing about Althea's daughter – not even her name. Only by uncovering the mysterious daughter's identity will the Order of the Owls get to the treasure and, perhaps, to Minerva's parents...

Chapter 1

A SHAMEFUL SHIPWRECK

Ravi was floating in a turquoise world with his eyes just half open. Dozens of fish danced around him, little white cottages dotted the coastline and a gentle breeze blew from the southwest. They were the ideal conditions for a nap, and he was already surrendering to sleep, when he saw a...

"SHARK!" Ravi yelled, almost dropping an oar.

"No, it's not, silly! It's just a sunfish," Thomasina said. She held a book about marine creatures on her lap. She had been studying the volume for a couple of days. "You see," she began to lecture, pointing at

the fish, "it's almost round in shape and floats in the water in a vertical position to get rid of parasites. It may be mistaken for a shark when only its dorsal fin emerges above the water."

"Well, that's exactly what happened. I saw the fin," Ravi said. He reached out to where the fish was with an unsteady hand but then stopped.

"Are you sure it won't bite?"

"It can't. It has no teeth," Thomasina replied.

"Come on, keep rowing!" Minerva urged him. "You had been doing so well before the, um, shark."

She sat in front of Ravi, next to Thomasina, and was nearly completely covered by a huge life jacket.

They all wore life jackets whenever they went out in the *Althea*. While Minerva and Ravi looked like two human hot dogs in theirs, Thomasina managed to wear hers with her usual grace. She had even customized it with a colourful lace trim. In case of a shipwreck, she had also added a watertight pocket to protect her brand new bag. (She had lost the old one back in the City of the Ravagers.) Her bag contained everything they needed for a new adventure.

Ravi lowered the oars into the water and thought that being forced to row was outright slavery. Why did he always have to do all the hard work?

A couple of seals that had been lazing on a rock, dove into the water and followed the boat's wake as it glided past them.

Thomasina studied them and leafed through her book, looking for the right page. "Here it is ... harbour seal ... *mammal of the Pinnipedia family...*"

The two seals were much faster than them, and after a while, as if tired of moving at a snail's pace, they sprinted ahead and vanished from sight.

"Ravi, are you going to let even seals pass you now?" Thomasina said.

"Well, if you don't mind, I'm the captain, and I choose the speed we keep," he snapped back.

Thomasina raised a perfectly curved eyebrow. "If you can call it *speed...*"

"I'm going slowly so that you can read without getting seasick," he explained. He fell silent, hoping to have had the last word. *Besides, I have to concentrate on the oars,* he said to himself.

Minerva had taught him how to row, but he needed much more practice. He never managed to

go straight, and every now and then, the boat jerked ahead or stopped abruptly, like a toad with a bad case of the hiccups.

Ravi would not run out of chances to practise, though. After they had found the boat, Minerva, who had the blood of pirates and navigators flowing through her veins, had decided that they were going to use it every single day.

She had finally convinced her friend to go back into the water, but it had taken a lot of effort, including making Ravi the captain.

"You have to overcome your limitations and defeat your fear," she had told him on the first day of rowing practice.

Ravi had to admit that rowing had helped him with his fear of water. Besides, sailing in a boat certainly had its moments...

Just like that one, when they tied the rope to a buoy off the coast of Pembrose, and he could put down the oars and enjoy a well-deserved rest.

He cleared his throat. "Ahem, because I'm the

captain," he began in an authoritative tone, "I order that we have a snack!"

"Wow! You're such a dictator!" Thomasina exclaimed, closing her book.

Ravi scowled at her. Why did she always have to use that sarcastic tone, especially as he had been madly in love with her since his first day at school in Pembrose? Besides, *she* was the real dictator!

Afraid that the usual squabble was about to break out, Minerva opened the basket that they kept in the bow. Empty stomachs increased the risk of fighting. "Who wants a cheese sandwich?" she asked.

"What else is in the basket?" asked Ravi, who would have preferred ten sandwiches.

"Lots of delicious things prepared by our French chef," Thomasina answered. She lived on a fancy estate with dozens of servants. "For her cheese sandwiches, Chef uses only true Brie and Camembert cheeses, which we have delivered directly from Paris. Thank you," she said, accepting the sandwich Minerva had handed her. "Did you know that sandwiches were invented by Lord Sandwich, an Admiral of the Royal Navy?"

"Really?" Ravi said, eyeing his friend's sandwich with new respect. If an admiral had invented it, he – as a simple captain – could do nothing but eat it. "May I have one, please?" he asked Minerva.

"He was a very busy man and had little time for lunch," Thomasina explained before graciously biting into her sandwich.

Her friends were much less delicate. Sea air made one very hungry, and they soon gobbled up the whole basketful of sandwiches. As far as eating speed was concerned, Ravi was sure he had honoured the inventive admiral.

At that point, they definitely needed a nap: Ravi lay on the floor of the boat and let the waves rock him gently. The clouds were tufts of candy floss, and the air smelt of salt and seaweed. Lured by the fish market, flocks of seagulls circled above the harbour. The sea was so clear that you could see schools of sardines passing by.

Ravi was just about to fall asleep, when Thomasina put the marine creatures book away and took out the diary where she kept notes about all their adventures. "If the captain will allow it," she said, gently nudging Ravi with her foot, "I would like to talk about the adventures that have been put on hold." A sly flame flickered in Thomasina's eyes: she was going to get her way, with or without his consent.

Ravi looked up at her, and the first thing that popped into his mind was that she looked beautiful even like that: upside down. He shook out of his trance, though, and almost told her to stop being such a pest.

A captain, however, must be kind to his crew, unless he wants a mutiny on his hands. "Okay," he said and sat up, yawning.

Minerva was happy to go over the recent developments too. Whenever they were in the boat, she couldn't help thinking about the City of the Ravagers, where they had found the vessel. The City of the Ravagers was an abandoned underground town that

they had discovered inside a huge cave underneath Admiral Rock. What's more, the boat's name was *Althea*, just like Minerva's ancestor, a beautiful and free-spirited woman who could control the elements.

Althea had been betrayed by the evil pirate Black Bart and was brought to die at the Tower of London. But before she met her dreadful fate, Althea had found a hiding place for her newborn baby girl, daughter of Merrival M., one of the Ravagers, whose portrait hung in Lizard Manor. She had left her daughter only two things: a powerful amulet to protect her and the only hint to the location of the Ravagers' treasure.

The problem was that Minerva and her friends didn't have a clue about what had become of the girl and the treasure.

Something had tickled Minerva's curiosity: Althea had signed her goodbye letter to Merrival using an owl-shaped wax seal with the words *Domina Noctuae* written on the edge. They had looked the words up in a Latin dictionary and had found out that it meant "Lady of the owls".

Minerva scratched her freckled, sunburned nose. *Could that have anything to do with the owls that live at Lizard Manor?* she wondered. What's more, their secret headquarters was in a place called Owl Tower. *An odd coincidence*, she thought.

Thomasina interrupted her trail of thought. "We have to find out what happened to Althea and Merrival's daughter," she decided.

"But she was born almost three hundred years ago," Ravi reminded her.

"It doesn't matter," Thomasina retorted. "Only by following her tracks will we get to the treasure and..."

"To my parents!" Minerva concluded, her eyes glistening.

She didn't talk about it much, but the idea of finding her parents never left Minerva.

Ravi sighed. He had a lot to think about while the waves cradled him.

"And let's not forget about this..." Minerva added, taking a crumpled piece of paper out of her pocket.

It was a letter written by someone who had signed himself "The Dragon". It was addressed to Minerva.

The girl read it out once more:

He who's found the key
and thinks himself wise
shall not rejoice for long,
for another'll get the prize!

That was it, just a couple of rhyming lines that sounded like a challenge to the Order of the Owls!

"Who do you think the Dragon is?" Thomasina asked.

Minerva shook her head. "It could be anyone in Pembrose."

"Who's been spying on us and knows that we've found the City of the Ravagers..."

"But not the treasure."

"One thing is certain: we can't trust anybody in the village."

Their conversation was interrupted when

Minerva noticed a shimmer coming from the harbour. "Someone's watching us with binoculars!" she cried. "But I can't see who it is," she said, squinting her eyes and shading them with her hand.

"Oh no! That must be Gilbert and his gang," Thomasina said. "They never leave us alone! Not for one second!"

"We're lucky they can't reach us here," Ravi said.

That was one of the perks of having a boat: you were safe from Gilbert's gang of bullies, who kept tormenting the Order of the Owls and all the other children in Pembrose and the neighbouring villages. However, how were they going to escape Gilbert's gang once they rowed back to shore?

They were all so concentrated on that thought that they were all caught off guard when a huge turtle rammed into their boat.

"Abandon ship!" was all Ravi managed to yell a second before the *Althea* capsized and they all fell into the water.

"What was that?" Thomasina asked, re-emerging next to him.

They all held onto the hull.

"A huge turtle hit us," Minerva answered. "It was lightning fast and disappeared just as suddenly."

"A turtle can't tip over a boat," Thomasina insisted.

Minerva, however, was absolutely certain that it had been a turtle.

Everything was possible in Cornwall.

Especially in Pembrose.

Chapter 2

THE MYSTERIOUS CABIN BOY

"What are we going to do now, Captain?" asked Thomasina.

"Well, we'll swim back to the harbour," Ravi answered. "It's not that far..."

"What about the boat?"

"We'll push it," Minerva interjected. She looked at Ravi. "Remember, the captain goes down with the ship," she scolded him.

So they headed for Pembrose, moving slowly, centimetre by centimetre. Minerva had taught Ravi how to swim, but he was still painfully slow. Even

the little crabs that crawled along the bottom were faster than their boat.

When they finally reached the shore, they were exhausted and dripping wet. Minerva had pieces of greenish seaweed hanging down her cheek. They beached the *Althea* and flopped down on the ground.

"Man, that was close!" Ravi panted.

"We were only a metre from the harbour, not exactly in the middle of the sea," Thomasina pointed out.

"Still, it was a remarkable feat!" said a voice behind their backs.

They whirled around and met a pair of dark, smiling eyes. They belonged to a young boy they had never seen before. He was dressed as a ship's cabin boy and wore a blue sailor's cap tilted over his forehead. The glint in his eyes made it clear that the stranger was making fun of them, and he wasn't even trying too hard to hide it.

That's who was spying on us! Minerva thought, noticing the binoculars hanging from his neck. "Who

are you?" she asked. She was always happy to meet new people and felt relieved not to be facing Gilbert, especially when the odds were so clearly against them.

"My name's Henry," he replied.

Was it just Minerva, or had the boy hesitated before answering? She thought she felt a light tickle on her toes, (her sign that someone was not being very honest) but it could have just been a tingle from the long swim.

"And why have I never seen you before?" a suspicious Ravi asked. He didn't like the boy's smirk.

"I only arrived a few days ago," Henry answered. "I'm on holiday."

"Are you staying at a bed and breakfast?" Thomasina asked.

Another hesitation. "Uh, yeah,"

Henry confirmed. "One not far from here," he added vaguely.

Minerva studied the boy's amber-coloured face. His big dark eyes betrayed no emotion, but he was definitely lying now. Her feet were tickling like crazy.

Before she could ask any other questions, though, the quiet of the village was shattered by a powerful trumpet call, followed by a trombone, a ghastly violin and a roll of drums. Finally an off-key chorus rose and struck up "Let Us Sail Away to the Sea". It was the most popular song in Pembrose.

Ravi covered his ears. "Oh, no," he grunted. "The Happy Fisherman Choir is rehearsing!" A small group of musicians and singers wearing Royal Navy uniforms had gathered on the wharf. "Come on, let's get out of here!" the boy decided, standing up.

They took off their life jackets and left them in the boat with the rest of their gear; thieves in a little village like theirs were unheard of. Ravi took only the picnic basket with him.

"Goodbye, Henry!" Minerva said.

"I hope I'll see you soon," Thomasina added.

Henry gave a perfect bow. "Glad to make your acquaintance, my lady!" he said with a charming smile.

"What a gentleman..." sighed an awestruck Thomasina.

In a fit of jealousy, Ravi grunted goodbye.

They made for the wharf, where, in addition to the usual bustle of the fish market, lots of things were happening. Actually, the whole village was full of activity: late July was peak season in Cornwall. In the narrow cobblestone streets, between white cottages and flowery windowsills, a group of volunteers was putting up decorations for the Seaman's Fest, one of the village's most cherished festivals. In the main square, Dr Gerald and Oliver, the village's only police officer, were giving the finishing touches to the fireworks. Meanwhile in the parsonage's garden, old Father Mullet and an eager group of local spinsters were making arrangements for the annual church raffle. Among the many familiar faces, the children

spotted Araminta Bartholomew and Ravi's mother talking with their friend Agatha, who was holding a basket full of the special medicines she made from the plants in the heath moor.

Plum Tree Avenue, the village's main street, was being blocked by Lola, a gentle pack horse that belonged to Timothy, owner of the Fishbone Inn, the only business of its kind in the village. Lola's little wagon was loaded with a new guest's luggage.

A lifelong resident of Pembrose, Timothy Long could be a handsome young man, if only he learned how to look less scruffy. First off, he could stop wearing those brown cardigans with elbow patches that he liked so much. Maybe then he would be less shy when he was around the lovely Gwendolyn Bartholomew, who never missed a chance to make eyes at him. Just then, the two of them were in the middle of an awkward conversation: Timothy was blushing red like a tomato, while the young shop owner looked incredibly charming as she held a pretty lilac parasol that shaded her porcelain white face.

"Hello, children!" said Timothy, jumping at the chance to interrupt Gwendolyn's attentions.

Gwendolyn immediately noticed that water was dripping from their clothes onto the ground. "What happened to you?" she asked.

"We were rammed by a giant turtle," answered Ravi. He was the captain, therefore he thought it was up to him to explain what had caused the shipwreck.

"Oh, my!" Gwendolyn exclaimed. "That must have been so scary!"

"Not at all," said Ravi, puffing out his chest as he tried to ignore Thomasina's taunting look.

"We were quite surprised to find such a big turtle swimming around here," Minerva butted in.

"Really unusual," Gwendolyn agreed. "What do you think, Timothy dear?"

The owner of the Fishbone blushed, and he looked as though he was about to choke. "I think you're wrong, children," he replied after a moment of uncertainty. And then turned as red as a beetroot. "There are no turtles around here. There never have been," he added decisively. "Excuse me, but I have to go now. Mr Coleman is waiting for his luggage." He pointed at his only customer, standing on the restaurant's doorstep.

Timothy grabbed Lola by the halter and walked away from them. He didn't even say goodbye to Gwendolyn.

The young woman was not hurt, though. It seemed as if she was used to his abrupt manners. She said goodbye to the children and made for the parsonage.

Minerva was thoughtful. She looked at the restaurant and its owner, feeling a terrible tickle on her toes. Something was not quite right.

"What is it?" Ravi asked.

Minerva ran a hand through her tangled red hair. "Did you see the look on Timothy's face when we told him about the turtle?"

Thomasina thought about it. "Yeah. His reaction was quite odd too," she admitted.

"Maybe we're just too suspicious," Ravi chimed in. At that point, all he cared about was going back home and slipping into dry clothes – not getting dragged into some more useless talk. "We've come to a point where it appears as if everyone has a secret. Give it some time, and I'm sure we'll even suspect Father Mullet of having something terrible to hide."

"To be honest, I didn't even see the turtle," Thomasina admitted.

"No, Timothy was lying," Minerva said with determination. "My toes were tickling..."

Ravi gave her a wary look: Henry was walking

their way once again. He must have followed them without them knowing. Now he was looking at them, his hands in his pockets and that street-smart grin on his face. "Do you want to know what I think about it?" he asked.

"Not at all," Ravi quickly retorted.

"I do," Minerva butted in, stepping right in front of Henry. She was still not sure what to think of him, and the two children looked at each other with challenge in their eyes.

Finally the boy held out his arms in sign of surrender. "All I wanted to say is that it really was a turtle that hit you. I saw it with my binoculars," he explained. "And it's not the first time that it has appeared here either. Therefore, your friend from the Fishbone is not telling the truth."

Neither are you, for that matter, Minerva thought. It wasn't yet time to expose him, though. What she wanted to do now was to find an explanation for Timothy's strange behaviour.

However, she didn't have time to think about it,

because they were interrupted by an old acquaintance of theirs.

"Old hag! Witch! Old crow!" a familiar voice called.

The children turned around. A tiny but extremely gifted parrot was fluttering around them.

"I don't believe it!"

"Napoleon!"

The parrot landed on Minerva's shoulder. "You're so ugly!" he gruffly said into her ear.

Minerva turned her head and met a pair of lively and feisty eyes. "What are you doing here?" she asked in a gentle tone.

"Crone!" Napoleon replied.

Ravi burst into laughter. "I'd say his trip to Brazil didn't make his mouth any sweeter!"

"Fleabag!" cried the parrot. Then to make sure he didn't leave out anyone, he turned to Henry. "You hideous creature!" he said to him.

"Henry, let me introduce you to Napoleon," Thomasina said, trying to stifle a giggle. "He's a Brazilian parrot. And Brazil is exactly where he

ought to be right now, as a matter of fact," she added, perplexed.

"I already know who he is," Henry replied. "He belongs to that woman over there." He pointed at Mrs Lavander, who was standing in the garden with the other raffle organizers. "She moved to Brazil to show Napoleon his native country, but she's come back to visit a friend," he explained. He smiled, obviously pleased by the fact that he knew so much more than they did.

Minerva looked at him with growing interest. Henry was a boy full of surprises. He could make an interesting friend. *First, I have to find out the truth about you, though,* she said to herself.

In the meantime, Napoleon had taken off. "See you around, ugly mugs!" he called. And he glided back onto his owner's shoulder.

"Mrs Lavander has a great tan," Thomasina observed. "Brazil was good to her."

"Mmm," Minerva nodded, but she wasn't listening. She was too busy observing the crowd of locals

who were hustling and bustling all over the place. The Dragon was hiding among them, and every single person was a suspect.

That's right, Pembrose looked just like one of the many pretty villages scattered around Cornwall. Things, however, are never what they seem...

Chapter 3

TURTLE ISLAND

Lizard Manor was exactly what it looked like: a huge fifty-five-room shack.

Sitting at the top of Admiral Rock, it had such a grim and threatening appearance that from a distance it looked like a bird of prey roosting in its nest, waiting to jump on its prey.

The house had been built with wood taken from sunken ships, which explained its odd shape. Years of neglect had definitely not helped. It was now so run down – with holes in the roof, burst pipes, bad electrical wiring, surly green-eyed portraits that

peeked at you from the walls, dust and spiders – that it seemed like the very last place a child would want to live. Minerva, however, felt snug and secure in that house. It didn't even matter that the mattresses were so damp that she couldn't even sleep in a real bed: her yellow tent was just perfect and was equipped with everything she needed.

Minerva was in her tent at that moment, sitting on the floor of the Tangerine Room, which took its name from the orange paint that was now peeling off the walls. It was Saturday morning, and she was studying a pile of books on marine animals that she had found in the library. Using the glow of an oil lamp, she turned each page with extreme care; they were so fragile that they might come apart at any moment. To help herself get in the mood for studying sea creatures, she had put on a mermaid costume, or rather, her interpretation of a mermaid costume: a long blue-green dress with a train that she had found in a trunk in the attic.

Hugo the badger kept her company. The animal

had been lured by the plate full of scones with jam that Minerva nibbled at as she read. The little animal had indeed developed quite a potbelly because of all his snacks.

"I've read enough!" Minerva decided, closing the last big book. "And you can finish the scones," she told Hugo, pushing the plate towards him. "I think it's almost time to go." She slid out of the tent, stretched, and leaned out of the window.

A light blinked in the distance: it came from Crowley Hall, Thomasina's home.

"Just as I expected!" Minerva exclaimed. "There's the signal!"

The Morse code signal meant: *Meet at the harbour in fifteen minutes.*

Minerva replied using the small mirror that she kept on the windowsill, pointing it towards the sun. *I'm on my way,* she signalled.

"Goodness! I have no time to waste!" she said to Hugo, who had popped out of the tent, his little snout covered with breadcrumbs.

In Minerva's rush to the door, she tripped on the train of the mermaid dress and fell facedown onto the floor. "Maybe I'd better change first," she decided.

She slipped into a short-sleeved shirt and a wrinkled skirt that she found in a trunk in the Tangerine Room and then ran down the dark stairs. "Goodbye Mrs Flopps!" she cried, darting past kitchen number three. Her guardian was making jams for the church raffle. Only the outline of her figure appeared behind the steam coming from the pots.

"I'll be back soon!" added Minerva. "I mean, I'll be back for dinner," she corrected herself. It was going to take her and her friends all day to do what she had in mind.

She hopped on her bike and, after a moment of hesitation, started down the shortcut that ran through Gilbert's turf. She had become such a great biker, she thought that she could escape any kind of attack.

Unfortunately, she paid no attention to the fourteen snowy owls roosting on the crooked chimneys

of the house. If she had, she would have noticed that they were rolling their yellow eyes as if to say, "Be careful."

"*Woot! Woot!*" hooted Augustus, the largest of the parliament. What he meant was, "Trouble ahead." Minerva, however, didn't hear him.

Unfortunately, Minerva had covered less than two metres when Gilbert and his best friend, Lucas, shot out from the side of the track, riding their Hurricane 1100 carbon mountain bikes.

"You won't get away now, Minerva Mint!" yelled her enemy.

Minerva managed to avoid them by swerving abruptly, then she pushed down hard on her pedals and yelled, "No, you don't, Gilbert!"

However, they were hot on her heels and would have gained on her if something extraordinary hadn't happened: a second after Minerva passed a point where the track was narrowed by two large rocks, a tight rope appeared out of the blue, and Gilbert and Lucas went flying in the air with their bicycles.

Henry came out from behind one of the rocks and called to Minerva. The girl went back for him, and he climbed on the bike, sitting behind her. Then she took off at full speed, leaving Gilbert and Lucas in the dust. The two boys were uninjured, but their bikes were too messed up to go after them. To make sure, however, Minerva sped to the village. Only when she could see the first houses did she turn to Henry. "Wow! That was close." She sighed. "Thanks for saving me! How did you know we'd come that way?"

Minerva was cycling so fast that Henry had to hold on tight to her, with his face pressed against her back, to avoid falling off. "I saw you coming down the road through my binoculars," he replied, lifting his head just a little. "Then I thought I should use the simplest trick: I tied one end of the line to one of the rocks..." he explained, "and hid behind the other one waiting for you to arrive. Then at the right moment, I pulled the line and ... *bawaaam!*"

"What were you doing out there?"

"I was exploring," said Henry with a shrug. "My

bed and breakfast is just over there," he added, pointing over to an area where there were only farmsteads.

Minerva's toes started to tickle, but she said nothing. She sort of liked the idea of a mysterious new friend. She also thought that, for the time being, there was no need to tell Ravi and Thomasina about her tickle: everything would be revealed in time.

The village was already buzzing with activity when they arrived in town. The narrow cobblestone alleys were teeming with volunteers, while the voices of Pembrose spinsters came from the parsonage's garden, interrupted occasionally by Napoleon who kept squeaking, "Crones!"

Minerva's bicycle stopped right at the edge of the pier, a few centimetres from the water and right in the middle of the rehearsing Happy Fisherman Choir, startling everyone.

"I'm so sorry!" said the girl, turning her bike around to go towards Ravi and Thomasina, who were waving her over from a secluded part of the harbour.

"What is *he* doing here?" Ravi immediately asked, pointing at Henry.

"He saved me from Gilbert," Minerva gleefully replied. She told her friends what had happened. "You should have seen what their new bikes looked like at the end!" she concluded with satisfaction.

"Wow," said Thomasina, looking at Henry with awe.

The boy pulled his hat down on his forehead and stuck his hands in his pockets. If it weren't for his cocky attitude, you might have thought that he was embarrassed.

"Oh ... well. Good for you," muttered an irritated Ravi. "Can we please get on with our plan now?"

"*Plan?*" asked Henry, intrigued.

Minerva thought about it for a minute, then she made up her mind. "As you saved me, we can tell you what's on our mind."

Unaware of Ravi's scowling, she told Henry that they had decided to follow Timothy to discover the reason for his strange behaviour.

Shortly after, they were waiting outside the Fishbone Inn, hiding behind Lola's cart. Whenever the innkeeper left for a time, they followed from a safe distance. For the most part, Timothy took care of terribly boring business: he went shopping, helped Dr Gerald and Oliver set up the fireworks, and came back and cooked lunch. At long last, when the gang were just about to give up hope, he did something very unusual. He slyly walked to a small hidden cove, not too far from the harbour. There, he climbed onto a motor boat and headed for Turtle Island, just off Admiral Rock.

"That's strange," said Minerva, putting down the binoculars that she had borrowed from Henry. "I wonder why he's going there."

Turtle Island was a sandy, windswept islet nobody ever went to because it stood exactly where several strong currents met.

"As a matter of fact," Thomasina said, "it is really odd of Timothy to go to Turtle Island after what he told us..."

"If it matters, he's been going there every single day since I arrived," Henry told them, shrugging his shoulders.

"What?" Ravi snapped. "Why didn't you tell us before?"

"I didn't want to spoil your fun," Henry replied. A devilish light flickered in his dark eyes.

Ravi looked sceptically at him. "Well, if you know so many things, then you must also know *why* Timothy has been going to the island."

Henry gave him an enigmatic smile. "I might..." he replied.

"What are you waiting for? Tell us!" an exasperated Ravi said.

Henry slowly looked at each one of them, then he seemed to give up. "Okay. But I want something in return."

Intrigued, Minerva scratched her nose. Were they about to unravel Henry's mystery?

"I want to join the Order of the Owls," he said. "At least for the time I'm here in Pembrose."

Ravi turned red with anger. "How do you know about the Order–"

Minerva nudged him. "It's a deal!" she interrupted to prevent any objection. She had decided that the bright boy would be a great addition to their group. "You're in." She shook Henry's hand.

* * *

Ravi did, in fact, raise several objections in his own way – that is, scowling at Minerva and grumbling non-stop. He was not okay with adding a new member to their secret club. It wasn't as if he was against the idea of extending the group exactly. He just didn't like Henry. Like Minerva, Ravi had come to the conclusion that he was hiding something.

Besides, Thomasina seemed crazy about the new boy, and that made Ravi insanely jealous.

A deal was a deal, though, so they went to the wharf and sat in their favourite spot, where they could take off their shoes and dip their feet in the cool water.

Henry sat in the middle and looked each of them in the eye. Then he began to speak. "I discovered what Timothy's been doing on the island two days ago when he came here with a biologist friend of his and ... well, I *accidentally* overheard their conversation," he explained, blushing, though it wasn't easy to see his face behind his tilted hat. "His friend brought him some special thermometers to measure soil temperature," he went on. "The friend said that they are used to check the sand temperature on the beach where the nests are–"

"The nests?" Thomasina interrupted him.

"That's right," Henry confirmed. "Inside the nest, there are eggs of a very rare kind of turtle," he explained. "It's called ... a blue turtle, I think. From what I heard them say, Timothy is taking care of the turtles nesting on the island all by himself, making sure that nothing happens to the eggs."

"Why is he doing it by himself?" Minerva asked.

"He doesn't want anyone to know, because the people from the village are a bunch of gossips,"

Henry replied. "He's afraid that if word gets out, thousands of tourists will swarm the island, which might disrupt the hatching. The blue turtle is an endangered species."

Minerva scratched her nose. "That's why Timothy told us that there were no turtles in this area," she said thoughtfully. "He didn't want us to know that they lay eggs on the island..."

"In front of Gwendolyn of all people," Ravi butted in. "Now there's a real gossip!"

"Mmm..." Minerva was thinking. "Blue turtle you said? Thomasina, look it up in your book!"

Her friend took out the manual on marine creatures from her bag, looked for the right page and read aloud: *"It is a very rare species, threatened by climate change, fishing nets and pollution. Close contact with man could result in its extinction."*

"Just like Timothy said," Ravi commented.

"A blue turtle may go as long as thirty years before it returns to its birthplace to lay its eggs, swimming in the sea for thousands of kilometres."

"Wow!" Ravi said, fascinated in spite of himself.

"Using their hind flippers, females dig out the holes where they deposit the eggs," Thomasina resumed. *"Then they cover them up to keep them warm and safe from the predators and finally return to the sea."*

"Timothy said that hatching time was close," Henry interrupted her. "And that this is the most delicate phase, in which the baby turtles must dig their way out of the sand. They wait for the night to come, because it is the safest time of day. Then they crawl back to the sea."

"How do they know when it's night?" Minerva asked.

Thomasina scanned the page. *"Hatchlings know that night has come when the sand cools down. Then, following the reflection of the Moon and the stars on the water, they journey to the sea."* All of a sudden she stopped and said, "Hey, I've got an idea. Why don't we go to the island to take a look?" she proposed. "Ravi, can you row all the way to the island with four people on board?"

Ravi gulped. "Four?"

"I'm obviously coming with you," Henry reminded him.

Ravi's face clouded over like the sky before a storm.

"Oh, yeah," Thomasina snorted. "Henry, first you have to ask the *captain* permission to board the *ship*."

Henry brought a hand to his forehead in a military salute. "Requesting permission to come aboard, captain."

"Yes, well ... I mean ... permission granted."

To avoid making a fool of himself in front of the newcomer once again, Ravi chose not to remind them that going out to the island meant going straight into a whirlpool of powerful currents. But like Minerva always said: Anything can happen, you just have to believe. Or so he hoped.

They got ready to leave. Fortunately there was a spare life jacket on the *Althea* for Henry. When they were ready, they pushed the boat into the water and climbed on board.

"Ready all, row captain!" Minerva shouted.

At that precise moment, they heard the noise of fluttering wings. "Full steam ahead, you bonehead!" Napoleon croaked, landing on Minerva's shoulder.

"Now the crew is all here!" Henry cried.

Truth be told, there was no way the descendant of a pirate could leave for a desert island without a foul-mouthed parrot as her companion. They truly were ready now.

"Starboard bow, Captain!" Minerva cried. "We're bound for Turtle Island!"

CHAPTER 4

A GOLDEN OMELETTE

Ravi had no idea how he managed to row all the way to the island without stopping even once. The only reasonable explanation was that he didn't want to look bad in front of Henry. When they finally arrived on the wind-lashed shore, however, he slumped facedown on the sand, unable to take another step.

"Come on, lazybones!" Thomasina urged as she walked down the beach next to Henry. "We must find the nests."

Ravi raised his head and thought about how life

was unfair: not one word of thanks, in spite of all his efforts!

"Wimp!" Napoleon cried from Minerva's shoulder.

"Do you need help getting up?" Minerva asked.

"Forget about it!" Ravi snorted, exasperated. He shot to his feet and rushed after Thomasina and Henry.

The perimeter of the island was one single long beach interrupted by dark granite rocks. The sand teemed with crabs, sea snails and shells, and in some points, where the currents were stronger, it was swept by a powerful riptide.

It didn't take them long to find what they were looking for. Thomasina spotted them first, helping herself with a photograph from her book. "Look," she said pointing at a dozen tiny sand dunes. "The nests!"

They kept their distance so they wouldn't upset the unhatched eggs. "It says here that each nest contains dozens of eggs," Thomasina said.

"How big are they?" Minerva asked.

"*The size of a ping-pong ball,*" Thomasina read.

Henry was looking at some footprints in the sand. "These must be Timothy's. They're all the same. That means that no one else has been here recently."

"Luckily," Ravi commented. He had begun to care for the little unborn turtles. He already felt like their protector.

Minerva, meanwhile, was staring at the sea, brooding. "Guys, we have to leave straight away!" she said. "If we don't, we'll never make it back to the harbour."

Only then did her friends realize that big dark clouds were approaching, pushed on by a wind that was rippling the water surface.

Without the slightest hesitation, they walked up to the boat and pushed it into the water. This time they took turns at the oars, and Henry surprised them all with his sailing skills. He could spot both dangerous currents and ones that would push them forwards, taking them to the harbour, safe and sound.

"That was close!" Ravi said once they had tied the *Althea* to a cleat. Then he remembered that he was the captain. "Good job." He surrendered to his rival in good sportsmanship.

In response, Henry tugged at his hat and pulled

it even lower over his forehead. "Thank you," he mumbled.

"So long, lazybones!" Napoleon said as he took off and headed back to his owner.

Minerva did not return the parrot's goodbye. She was lost in thought.

"We have to go to Timothy and offer our help," she said at last. "He can't take care of everything by himself, especially now that he has his hands full with the festival preparations."

The others agreed, and so they set out for the inn.

"Is anybody here?" asked Minerva as she opened the door.

The restaurant's main room, with its saltwater-soaked dark wood panelling, was empty. That was not all that unusual though: the Fishbone was an old quaint inn, but it was without modern conveniences, like hot water and central heating. As if that wasn't bad enough, Timothy's homemade fish delicacies were guaranteed to give his patrons a three-day stomach-ache.

"Let's sit down and wait for him," Henry said.

The children sat in one of the wooden booths, typical of a traditional inn. They immediately heard someone talking on the restaurant's pay phone that hung on the wall right behind them. It wasn't Timothy.

They all hid down in their seats.

"It must be Mr Coleman," Thomasina whispered. The Fishbone had only one room, so it couldn't have been anyone else.

"No, nobody suspects me. Don't worry, Ben," the voice said.

The children cowered at the sound of those words and exchanged puzzled glances.

"Our friend Robin's tip was right on the money. The blue turtles are nesting on the island," the man reported.

The children's ears pricked up.

"And the eggs are going to hatch in a couple of days," the voice continued. "I know because that dimwit innkeeper has been taking care of them, though he thinks no one knows about it... I think it's

almost time by the way he's been behaving... No, don't worry about him. He won't mess with us, and if he does, I know what to do, you have Alfred Coleman's word..."

Ravi shuddered: it *was* Mr Coleman, and he sounded lik e a terrible man!

"Not a chance, I tell you," the man insisted, trying to reassure the person on the other end of the line. "You've got to be kidding. That idiot doesn't even realize the goldmine he's sitting on... He hasn't the slightest clue of how much those

eggs are worth... We'll sell them to wealthy food fanatics. They are so rare that they'll be ready to pay a king's ransom to be able to make themselves a nice blue turtle egg omelette."

Ravi couldn't help himself. "Yuck!" he said in disgust.

"Hush!" Minerva said.

"I'll go and hire a boat now," Coleman said. "I'll talk to you later, as soon as I've come up with a plan."

The children waited until the man had left and then they re-emerged from under the table, where they had slipped for fear of being seen.

Ravi was disgusted. "What kind of people are these?" he cried. "Have you ever heard of people that eat turtles' eggs?"

Thomasina was consulting her book. "Unfortunately, yes," she replied. "It says here that they are considered a delicacy. And, because selling them is illegal, the 'connoisseurs' are ready to pay big money to get their hands on them."

The four children exchanged dismayed looks.

"One thing's for certain," Minerva finally said. "We can't ask for Oliver's help. You know what he's like."

The brawny village police officer was not used to carrying out investigations in a town where crimes were rarely committed. He would just make a mess of it, like the time the Order of the Owls was investigating Black Bart the pirate.

"And now that we know that real criminals are involved in this, we can't even tell Timothy," Minerva continued. "He's not exactly what you would call coolheaded: he'd panic, and Coleman would find out that we're on to him in a matter of hours. Timothy has his restaurant to look after, so he can't watch the eggs all day. But we can," she concluded, looking at her friends.

"That's right!" Thomasina said. "We'll protect the eggs twenty-four hours a day until they hatch. And we'll teach that crook a lesson! This sounds like the perfect mission for the Order of the Owls, don't you think?"

Ravi was okay with the general idea of the plan,

but there was one detail that the others seemed to be neglecting. "How are we going to be able to stay on the island for a couple of days without telling our parents and Mrs Flopps?"

"I can answer that," Henry chimed in. "I have a plan."

He had been so silent up to that moment, that Ravi had almost forgotten about him. "Oh yeah?" he asked sceptically. "What kind of plan?"

"Well, it so happens that my parents have signed me up for a three-day camping trip with a scouting club."

At these words, Minerva's toes started to tickle, but she decided not to interrupt the boy. She wanted to know what he had in mind.

"The bus leaves from Pembrose main square tomorrow morning. Here's my plan: you could ask your parents' permission to go camping. It gives you the perfect excuse to get all the stuff we're going to need on the island," he explained. "And nobody will suspect a thing when we show up in town with

our rucksacks and sleeping bags," he added with a grin. "It goes without saying that you three won't sign up for real, and I'll cook up an excuse for the scout leader and pull out at the very last moment."

Thomasina clapped her hands. "That's so clever!" she cried out. "We'll have three days all to ourselves."

"Good! Hopefully that will be enough time for the eggs to hatch," Minerva said. She too seemed to approve of that plan.

Ravi himself would have approved, if only he hadn't been jealous of the head-over-heels expression on Thomasina's face whenever she looked at that Henry. A mumbled "okay" was all he managed.

Minerva was ecstatic now. "Tomorrow we'll take over the island, and we'll keep everybody else away until the young turtles have reached the sea."

"Hooray!" Thomasina cheered.

"The church raffle is tomorrow morning," Henry added. "We'll have a chance to leave unnoticed while it's being drawn."

"You're a genius!" Thomasina said.

Ravi felt a terrible jab of jealousy: the pain was so great that he turned white.

Minerva noticed and looked for a way to cheer him up. "You wanna know something?" she whispered to him while Henry and Thomasina discussed the gear they'd need on the island. "Henry is not what he seems. Not all he says is true."

A little bit of colour came back on Ravi's face. "Are you sure?" he whispered.

Minerva nodded and pointed at her feet.

"They've tickled a lot?" Ravi whispered, full of hope.

"A little," Minerva replied.

Ravi clenched his jaw and decided that he would keep a close eye on that Henry, and at the right moment, he would unmask the boy right in front of Thomasina, making a terrific impression on the girl he adored!

Chapter 5

SEA DOGS

The following day the members of the Order of the Owls met behind the small village church exactly as the clock tower struck ten. They were carrying rucksacks and camping gear and wearing hiking clothes.

All but Thomasina.

Ravi stared at her with dreamy eyes. It occurred to him that though she didn't look one bit like a scout, she was very beautiful. She was wearing a spotless high-collared shirt with a bow tie, a velvet,

tight-waisted blouse and a pair of matching trousers. A pretty little hat was propped to the side on her blonde head.

Henry shook Ravi out of his daydream and yanked him back to reality. "I've told the scout leader that I wouldn't be able to join them," he said, pointing at a big bus parked in the square opposite the church.

Dozens of boys and girls wearing shorts were gathering round it.

Minerva felt an unbearable tickle on her toes and had to stifle a giggle.

Ravi noticed her discomfort and studied his rival's face, but the boy's expression gave nothing away.

"Did you have any problem asking for your parents' permission?" Henry asked.

"My mum was happy for me to go camping," Ravi replied.

Because she and Ravi had recently arrived from India, Mrs Kapor thought that the trip would be a good opportunity for Ravi to make new friends.

Minerva ran a hand through her curly hair. It was more tangled than usual – probably a sign of the upcoming adventure. "I don't think Mrs Flopps could exactly hear me this morning when I asked her if I could go. She was too busy filling up the last jam jars for the raffle. But she said yes."

In that moment, all eyes were on Thomasina. Her parents were respected members of the British aristocracy, and camping was definitely not on their list of favourite activities.

"Oh, not a problem!" the girl said, shrugging her shoulders.

Ravi was particularly surprised. "Really?"

"Well, I didn't *exactly* use the term *camping*..." Thomasina admitted. She flashed a smile. "You know, I twisted the story a little bit and asked my parents if I could take part in a three-day fox hunt."

Ravi was amazed by her cleverness. There was nothing that Sir Archibald and Lady Annabelle Crowley loved more than fox hunting.

"So they immediately granted me permission to go with no questions asked," Thomasina concluded.

"Very clever!" Henry said.

"I agree!" Thomasina twirled, holding her hat in one hand. "This is my Amazon outfit. Do you like it?"

"Well, it's not ideal for sailing..." Ravi grumbled. He hadn't liked the looks Thomasina had exchanged with that fellow Henry.

"Oh, I almost forgot! I have some luggage," Thomasina added, stepping aside and revealing a pile of suitcases.

They looked terribly heavy, and Ravi suspected that he would be the one in charge of carrying them to the boat. "Did you really have to bring all this stuff?" he snorted.

"Just the bare necessities," the girl protested. "This blue suitcase contains the sea adventure books that we'll read at night before going to sleep. In the little pink suitcase, I have the nautical charts, a sextant, a battery radio, torches and parachute flares. In the red one, I put everything we need to set up traps, and in the green one, there are oilskin jackets, sleeping bags, boots and other pieces of basic clothing. *This* is indispensable," she said, showing them the compass that she kept around her neck. Then she held up her trusted bag. "And here I have our diary and other useful things."

"Well, I guess we're ready to go!" exclaimed a pleased Minerva.

Hidden behind Father Mullet's lush rosebushes, the children waited for the bus to leave. Then they witnessed the arrival of the villagers, who filled the

parsonage garden. They were all happy and excited at the idea of the upcoming raffle.

"We've almost made it," Henry whispered.

Ravi eyed the boy. He was dressed like a scout with his hat tilted over his lively dark eyes. Ravi had to admit that, though a big liar, Henry did have his act together. In fact, everything was going according to plan. They remained hidden until they heard Father Mullet announce that he was about to draw the name of the first winner.

"We have to go," Henry whispered. "Today's weather report forecasted rough sea, starting at noon."

Ravi picked up his rucksack and all of Thomasina's suitcases and trudged after the others to the wharf. Fortunately, the streets were empty.

Once they had finished loading the *Althea*, the little boat was so full that it almost sank.

The gang put on their life jackets and went aboard.

"Hold on!" Henry stopped them. "One last thing." He flashed one of his wise-guy smirks and took out

two large rags from his pockets, which he put into the oarlocks. "This way we won't make a sound," he explained. "It's going to work, trust me."

And work it did. When Ravi put the oars into the water, the gentle lap of the sea was all you could hear.

"Stop at once, ye rascals!" a loud, furious voice suddenly cackled.

The four friends jumped, afraid that they had been discovered. However, it was just Napoleon.

The little parrot perched on Minerva's shoulder and scowled at the girl. "You old crone!" he told her.

"Oh, I had no idea you wanted to come along," Minerva apologized. "Anyway, don't say a word until we're out of earshot," she warned him, "or they're going to find us."

True to his sea parrot nature, Napoleon kept silent. But once they were far from the harbour, he croaked, "Shrinking violets!"

The children knew that they had made it: a new adventure for the Order of the Owls had begun!

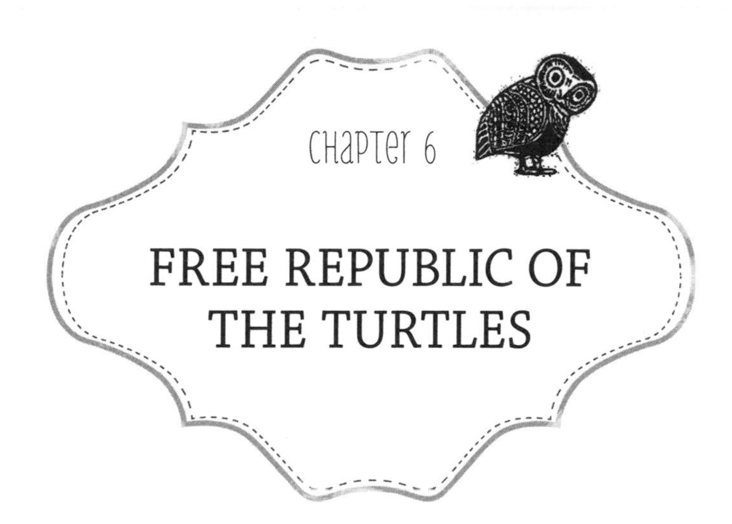

Chapter 6

FREE REPUBLIC OF THE TURTLES

"Somebody saw us leave," Henry said once they had set foot on the island.

"Who?" Ravi asked as he piled up Thomasina's monstrously heavy suitcases. By then, it was clear to him that *captain* was just another word for servant.

The *Althea* was so full that beaching it would have been impossible. Therefore, Ravi and Henry had unloaded everything while Minerva and Thomasina held the boat still in the shallow water.

After commenting on their efforts with a loud

"Layabouts!" Napoleon had shot off to take a look around on his own.

"Your friend Gilbert was watching us," Henry replied. "When I looked with my binoculars, I saw him on the edge of the Pembrose peninsula. I didn't tell you before because I didn't want to spoil the trip," he explained.

"*Ugh!*" Minerva snorted. "I knew he wouldn't leave us alone."

"So now we'll have to watch out for his gang *and* for Mr Coleman." Ravi sighed. "If he gets his hands on a boat, we'll be trapped."

"Don't worry," Minerva reassured him, her green eyes glittering with a fighting light. "We are going to give our guests a warm welcome!"

"What have you got in mind?" asked Ravi. He knew that light, and he knew that it meant big trouble. *For him*.

"You'll see..." the girl replied, winking. "First off, we must hide the *Althea* so no one will know we're here." She looked about. "Mmm, let's drag it under

those bushes over there." She pointed to where the grass and plants grew nearly to the water's edge.

Ravi and Thomasina pulled the boat, while Henry and Minerva pushed it. They were lucky that the boat was small enough to fit under the bushes.

That done, the children took off their life jackets and left them in the boat.

"Very well." Minerva caught her breath. "Let's explore the island now and decide where we want to set up our camp. This way!" she exclaimed, darting into a maze of lush, red flowers. Her friends had to rush after her to keep up.

They felt like they were walking through a jungle, and it was obvious that no one had been inland for several years. At the end of a long and tiring walk, they finally reached the highest point: a stony peak that overlooked the whole island.

They took turns with the binoculars, scanning the coastline that snaked its way before them. The steep granite cliffs were so ragged and pointy that it looked like they had been cut out with an axe.

If you shifted the binoculars towards the open water, the landscape was even wilder. Ruthless winds swept furiously across that stretch of sea, and the bottom was probably littered with the wrecks of dozens of sunken ships. Murders of crows and flights of cormorants flew continuously over the area, patiently waiting for a disaster to happen.

"Hey! There's something over there!" Ravi exclaimed. "They look like ruins."

"Let me see!" Thomasina snatched the binoculars from his hands. "You're right! Let's go and have a look." She looked at her compass. "Southwest, forward, march!"

They followed a winding, stony path to a peak that was not as high as the first one, but definitely more secluded. In fact, it was invisible from the beach. Someone had built a real fort there. The roof had collapsed, but the walls, though crumbling, were still there, along with a vine-covered tower.

Minerva rushed to the tower and scanned the area. "I have no idea who built this," she said,

"but they did us a big favour. This place provides great protection. We'll put up our tent right here," she decided.

Henry and Ravi dug a hole in the sand and put the water bottles in it to keep them cool. They laid out the sleeping bags, put up a tent and gathered kindling for the fire, laying it in the middle of a ring of stones.

Thomasina pulled the books out of the blue suitcase and carefully laid them next to her sleeping bag, while Minerva, who was in charge of the food supplies, emptied her rucksack.

Ravi looked at her with surprise. "Don't tell me you only brought strawberry jam!" he blurted out.

Minerva smiled. "That's right. It's ideal food to survive on a desert island, don't you agree? Jam lasts a long time and provides a lot of energy."

Ravi grimaced, feeling sick already. He couldn't say anything else, though, because Henry, who had been examining the inside of the fort, called out to them. "Hey you lot, I've found a freshwater well!"

The well was a hole dug into the ground. Henry had pulled up the bucket using the pulley system. “Someone probably lived here at one point, if they needed water,” he said.

“That could be,” Minerva agreed. “The most important thing now, however, is that we won’t need to ration the bottles of water we brought with us.”

“Who do you think built this fort?” Ravi asked. The place had an eerie feeling of abandonment.

“It looks very old,” Thomasina replied. “Maybe, back in the day, it was used by coastguard soldiers to fend off pirates and smugglers’ attacks.”

“Or maybe it was a hideout used by criminals!” Henry guessed, much more excited by his hypothesis.

“Well, it’s *ours* now,” Minerva said. “Follow me, I have a surprise to show you.”

The others followed her to the clear space where they had put up their tent. She took something out of her rucksack and swiftly hid it behind her back. “In order to make our ownership of the fort official, we’re going to use this!” she exclaimed. She unrolled

a big blue flag on which she had written in huge letters: *FREE REPUBLIC OF THE TURTLES*.

Thomasina clapped her hands. "It's beautiful!"

Minerva gloated. "I made it last night. You know, sea people always state who they are," she explained. "It's a rule."

"Just like pirates do with the Jolly Roger." Henry was thrilled. "The flag with the skull and crossbones!"

They tied one end of the flag to the top end of a long branch and drove it into the sand. Then they stood there for a moment, admiring the flag flapping in the wind. Although the hardest part of the adventure was still ahead of them, they felt very proud of what they had accomplished so far.

One crew member was missing out on the flag-raising ceremony, but he quickly joined his friends. Fluttering his wings, Napoleon perched on top of the pole and squawked: "Come on you layabouts!"

Led by Thomasina, who never took her eyes off the compass, the children completed a full lap around

the island and finally came to the exact point where the turtle eggs were.

The little dunes were untouched, and the wind had swept away the footprints in the sand. No one had been there since the day before.

Ravi kneeled down and carefully examined one of the nests. He couldn't fathom the fact that many little lives were right under that sand, ready to come out. "How are the turtles going to make it out on their own?" he wondered aloud. "They must be so small."

Thomasina consulted the book on marine creatures that she was still carrying in her bag. *"Upon hatching, a blue turtle measures less than five centimetres,"* she read.

"That small?" Minerva said, bewildered. "Can't we just help them out then?"

Thomasina shook her head. "It says here that they must not be touched. And we can't help them reach the sea either – they have to make it on their own. It's how the hatchlings develop an internal compass that they'll need when they're in the sea."

Ravi put his ear close to the sand and almost felt as if he could hear many little heartbeats. "Come on, little ones!" he whispered.

Thomasina was still reading the manual. "Once they have reached the sea, the newborn turtles will swim for a whole day without stopping, but they'll always remember where they were born, and many years later they will return to that place to lay their eggs," she said. "How they manage to find the exact spot is one of nature's mysteries."

Minerva looked at the dunes and thought that she would do all she could to protect them: a mystery of nature is a very important thing to preserve.

As they had skipped lunch, the children decided to have a snack on the beach. Minerva took out four jam jars and four spoons from her rucksack. "Enjoy!" she said happily.

Her friends were too hungry to be picky, but after a couple of spoonfuls they had had enough. Luckily, Thomasina had some chocolate biscuits in her bag.

Napoleon snatched a biscuit and then took off,

looking for something else to peck on. "So long, wimps!" he said.

Ravi decided to follow his example. "I want to catch a nice fish for tonight's dinner," he said.

"You know how to do that?" Thomasina asked.

Ravi puffed out his chest. "Of course I do! All I need is a branch and a length of rope. We have plenty of both."

"What are you going to use as bait?" Henry asked.

"Well, I don't know yet," Ravi admitted. "A worm, I suppose..."

"What about the hook?"

Ravi didn't answer. As a matter of fact, he had no clue what do about the hook.

"Don't worry, my friend, I'll help you!" Henry exclaimed, giving him a pat on the back.

Ravi was about to tell him that he didn't need any help when the battery radio that was tuned to a local station suddenly crackled. *"Force 12 winds and strong winds from Scandinavia... Boating activities are strongly discouraged until tomorrow afternoon..."*

Minerva grinned. "Perfect, we won't have visitors for a while," she said, pleased. "And then tomorrow morning, we'll have all the time we need to prepare a warm welcome for Gilbert and Coleman!"

Ravi noticed the fighting look on her face, and in it he saw a reflection of her ancestors, the Ravagers of the Sea, and of Minerva, the war goddess she was named after. Gilbert and Coleman had better keep their eyes peeled!

* * *

Henry made fishing rods for everyone using branches and pieces of rope. He pulled a couple of sweets out of his pocket and tied one on the end of each line.

"It's liquorice," he said. "The fish will think they're flies and bite."

He showed the others how to cast a line with a nimble movement of his wrist.

"Wow, where did you learn to do that?" an amazed Thomasina asked him.

They were standing on a rock lashed by waves that were getting taller as the Nordic winds grew stronger.

Henry hesitated. "My father taught me," he finally answered.

Ravi immediately looked at Minerva and noticed that she had put a hand over her mouth to stifle a laugh. *Another lie!* he thought. Henry was something else.

Ravi casually cast his line, while keeping an eye on his rival, and so he was caught by surprise when he felt a powerful tug. "I got something!" he shouted. "Help me! Something huge is pulling me in!"

"Let it go!" Minerva said.

"Not a chance!" replied a stubborn Ravi.

Henry grabbed him by the waist and pulled with all his strength. The boys fell back, uninjured, and Ravi's rod snapped. Furious, the boy turned to complain, but the words died on his lips.

In the fall, Henry's hat had caught in a thorny bush, exposing a flow of long, jet-black hair.

"Y-you a-are ... a girl!" Ravi stammered.

"Oh, my goodness!" Minerva exclaimed. That's why her feet had been tickling so much!

The girl ran a hand through her shiny hair and smiled apologetically. "I knew you would find out sooner or later," she sighed. "At this point I guess I can tell you that my name is Henrietta."

"But ... why do you dress up as a boy?" Thomasina asked.

Henrietta shook her head. "I'm sorry, but I can't tell you that yet," she said. "I promise I'll tell you everything before I leave Pembrose." She looked pleadingly at them – her confidence seemed to disappear the moment her secret was exposed. "Can I still be a member of the Order of the Owls?" she asked.

Ravi, Minerva and Thomasina exchanged looks. Ravi was happy that Henry – Henrietta, that is – was no longer a rival. However, with all those girls around, he'd be outnumbered. The other two were already more than enough to drive him crazy.

But then he realized that Henrietta was looking at them, her eyes full of hope, and his gentleman's heart could not resist. "Okay," he said with a sigh.

* * *

That night, sheltered in the fort so that no one could see them from the coast, the children built a crackling fire and roasted four big fish. Millions of stars shone in the sky next to the crescent Moon so thin that it looked like it had been painted with the

stroke of a paintbrush dipped in silver. It was warm inside their shelter, and the raging sea around them provided protection from any outside danger.

While they ate, Minerva, Ravi and Thomasina told Henrietta about the adventures of the Order of the Owls: how they had found Merlin's real cave and the City of the Ravagers. They told her about Black Bart's fabled treasure and Althea the witch, one of Minerva's ancestors. They also talked about the secret of Minerva's origins.

Their new friend listened closely, her mouth hanging open. "Wow," she exclaimed at last. "I had no idea Cornwall was such an exciting place."

"Ravi didn't either," Thomasina commented. "But he has changed his mind."

The boy blushed. "Well, sometimes it's a little *too* exciting," he mumbled.

The three girls burst into laughter, and in the end, he joined them. Happiness was contagious in that atmosphere, sitting around the fire, their bellies full and a great sense of joy just for being there, together.

"What about a little music?" Henrietta suggested.

"Crank it up, baby!" Napoleon croaked from Minerva's shoulder.

"As you wish, sir," Henrietta said, laughing.

She had done up her hair in a practical ponytail, and now that they were no longer hidden under the hat, you could clearly see her high cheekbones and smooth skin. Her eyes, however, were her most amazing feature, and they glittered as she took out a harmonica from her pocket. She put it to her lips and started playing.

"Wow, you're great!" Minerva exclaimed. Then she stood up, took Ravi and Thomasina by the arms, and pulled them into a crazy dance. At one point, she even started singing "Let Us Sail Away to the Sea" and other songs she had learnt from the fishermen at the top of her lungs.

They spent the night that way: with music and songs around the fire, just like real sailors.

When they felt so tired that they could no longer stand, they slipped into their sleeping bags, which

were laid around the smouldering embers. Like that, looking at the sky, they discovered a new world.

"That's Polaris," Henrietta said, raising a finger in the direction of a tiny, glimmering speckle very, very far away. "You use it to work out which way's north, and it helps navigators keep their route at all times."

"How do you know so much about the sea?" Ravi asked her.

"It's a secret," Henrietta sighed, crossing her arms behind her head as she watched the great spectacle of the heavens. "A secret I will soon reveal to you..."

"Are you ready for a bedtime story?" Thomasina asked, opening one of her adventure books. "It's about a pirate crew and their ship, the *Dame in Black*, who terrorized the inhabitants of the islands of the China Seas. The captain was a one-eyed man by the name of Cut-throat Jack..."

Ravi closed his eyes, cradled by Thomasina's voice and by the lapping of the waves. *What a wonderful way to fall asleep,* he thought one instant before he fell into a deep slumber.

Chapter 7

LET'S BOARD!

The huge pirate was looking at him with a murderous sneer. "Yer done now, bilge rat!" he growled, baring his teeth. His left cheek was crossed by a scarlet-coloured scar; doubtless the mark left by a sabre.

"No! Mercy!" Ravi yelped, sitting up in the sleeping bag. He was glad that it had only been a dream.

It was a beautiful sunny day, but you could still hear the roar from the sea at the bottom of the hill. Ravi smiled: it meant no visitors for the time being.

The girls were still sleeping, so he decided to take a stroll around the ruins. He took a couple of chocolate biscuits from Thomasina's bag and crossed the half-collapsed bridge, whistling softly. It was definitely a very old building. The stones had been smoothed by the wind and rain and were covered in vines and weeds.

Napoleon, a real early bird, came back from one of his reconnaissance flights and landed upon a wall. "Hairy ape!"

"Hi, Napoleon. Would you like a biscuit?" Ravi kindly offered, standing on the tip of his toes to reach up to the bird.

The parrot snatched the biscuit out of his hand and flew away. The boy lost his balance and fell forwards against the wall, which, instead of breaking his fall, moved. "Help!" he yelled, falling head first into a dark room.

Awoken by the scream, the girls immediately rushed over and found him lying on the ground, still wondering what had happened.

Thomasina scowled at him. "How dare you discover things without us?" she said.

"Actually..." Ravi tried to retort.

No one was listening to him, though, because Thomasina had just turned on the torch she kept in her bag, revealing the interior of a secret room.

"Whoa!" Minerva exclaimed.

In front of them there were spades, pickaxes and all kinds of other tools, coils of rope, ladders, two small catapults and a barrel full of a glowing yellow powder.

Minerva took a pinchful of the powder and smelt it. "Mmm, smells like glue," she said. "Thomasina, shine a light on the barrel please!"

The light beam exposed a tag that read: *Add water, roll into balls and hurl.*

On the lid was an unrolled scroll. Thomasina shone the light on it, and they all craned forwards to look. It was a map of the island: a series of points had been marked with crosses, and next to each cross was an apparently meaningless word.

"What do you think that's for?" a puzzled Ravi asked.

"Maybe it shows where treasure is hidden," Henrietta suggested.

"Of course!" Thomasina agreed. "Buried by the buccaneers who had sought shelter here."

"Let's investigate right now!" Minerva decided. "There's a cross right here at the bottom of the fort."

They reached the point marked on the map. It was a small bridge that hung over a little gorge.

Minerva ran a hand through her curls made frizzy by wind and the salty air. She looked at the map and then turned her eyes to the bridge. "It says 'Rope' under the bridge," she said pointing at the word. "I get it now!"

She fumbled through the bushes at the beginning of the bridge and found a rope. When she pulled it, the bridge opened up right in the middle.

The other three were amazed.

Minerva was overjoyed. "Don't you get it? This isn't a treasure map: it shows the traps used to

defend the fort," she explained. "Bravo, Ravi! You made a discovery that has made things much easier for us!"

"Actually ... I mean..." the boy stammered. "It's all a matter of instinct," he concluded.

"All we have to do now is make sure that the traps still work and fix the ones that don't," Minerva said. "Then we'll be ready for Gilbert and Coleman!"

The children spent the whole morning looking for the points marked on the map: they found many snare traps with nooses tied to tree limbs and piles of rocks ready to crumble and roll over the unlucky person that triggered their mechanism. There were also plenty of holes covered in twigs and leaves. They were very lucky that they had not fallen into any of those ancient traps the day before.

Minerva peered through the little twigs that covered the biggest hole and smiled.

"What's in there?" asked Ravi, worried.

"You had better not look," she answered. "This one's for our friend Gilbert."

After a snack made up of chocolate biscuits and jam, they got back to work. They made gluey balls by adding water to the glowing yellow powder and set up a series of catapults and ammunition at two strategic points.

Minerva designed an ingenious alarm system for the beach of turtle nests: a very thin fishing line pulled tightly over the sand. If someone coming from the sea happened to step on it, they would set off a number of little bells fixed to one end of the line that went all the way up to the fort.

"You gave me the idea for this, Henrietta," Minerva explained, "when you saved me from Gilbert. So I brought a fishing line and some bells with me."

The memory of that victory brightened her new friend's eyes. "Good thinking!" she said.

Pleased with themselves, the gang thought about what they had accomplished.

"The little turtles are safe now," Minerva said.

Ravi crouched down on the sand to look closely at a dune. He hoped to catch a glimpse of movement

that would tell him that the tiny turtles were about to crawl out of their eggs. "Come on, little ones!" he whispered.

In the meantime, the sea had grown calmer. There was only a light breeze, barely strong enough to ruffle the treetops.

Minerva was the first one to notice. She scanned the smooth expanse of water and sighed. "Everyone, from now on we must keep our eyes wide open."

The others nervously followed her glance.

"Everything will go according to our plans," she tried to reassure them. "Remember, we have a big advantage over Coleman: he doesn't know anything about us. And as far as Gilbert is concerned–"

At that exact moment, Napoleon plunged on them. "Scoundrels! Traitors! Rogues!" he croaked.

"It seems he's here," Minerva concluded.

They went up to the fort and looked around with the binoculars. Gilbert, his partners Damian and Lucas, and his mastiff, William the Conqueror, were climbing out of their boat on a small beach that

was on the opposite side with the turtle nests. They looked ferocious and determined. Especially Gilbert.

The battle was about to begin.

Minerva gave the binoculars back to Henrietta and drew a deep breath. "Are you ready?" she asked the others. Her freckled little face was firm and determined.

"Yes!" they answered in unison.

"Hands to action stations!" she yelled. "*Gooooo!*"

They dashed to the beach so that the gang could see them. Then on Minerva's signal, they pretended

to run away scared. They had already decided what way to go, with plans to set all the traps marked on the map.

"Look at that! They're running away!" Gilbert exclaimed triumphantly. "They're scared of us!"

"What a load of chickens!" Damian laughed at them.

"Ha-ha! They're a load of babies!" Lucas shouted.

"Minerva Mint," Gilbert bellowed, "you're mine now!"

William the Conqueror bared his teeth and was the first to run after them.

"Chaaarge!" howled Gilbert, following the dog.

They followed the Order of the Owls into the thick of the woods until – *Splat! Splat! Splat!* – they were hit square in the face by mushy glowing yellow balls. Even William the Conqueror got hit in the snout.

Half-blinded by yellow goo that had remained stuck to their eyelids, the attackers resumed their pursuit more furiously than before.

"You won't get away!" roared Gilbert, running

with his arms stretched out in front of him to make his way through the plants. "As soon as I get you, I'll make you all pay for this!"

On the contrary, just like Minerva had predicted, they ran straight into one trap after another.

They fell into the gorge in the middle of the bridge, plummeted through a series of holes and stepped straight into the snare traps.

What's more, they had to deal with Napoleon, who kept attacking them, pecking at their noses and squawking "Fools! Apes! Wimps!" Finally, blinded and covered in dirt and leaves, they walked straight into Minerva's final surprise.

"Help! Something's crawling on my face!" Lucas yelped.

"It's creeping up my leg!" howled Gilbert.

"Do you give up?" Minerva asked, leaning over the hole. Her face, framed by red curls, opened in a big smile. "I'd like to inform you that you've just fallen into the nest of a very rare kind of poisonous millipede. If we don't get you out of there in a few

minutes, you'll end up covered in festering boils and spend the rest of your days scratching like mad."

Of course, that wasn't true: it was just a bunch of fat earthworms, but the enemy didn't know that.

"Well?" Minerva pressed them. "You've got ten seconds left before I take back my offer ... nine ... eight ... seven ... six..."

"All right!" Gilbert squealed. "We give up!"

"Yeah! We give up!" yelled Damian. "Get us out of here!"

"Do it now!" Lucas screamed. "I don't want a scratch for the rest of my life."

"Hooray!" Henrietta cheered. "The girl gang won! Oops, I'm so sorry, Ravi."

Though he was the only boy in the group, Ravi was so happy for that victory that he didn't mind being the minority.

They lowered a ladder into the ditch and let out their three enemies and William the Conqueror. A miserable Gilbert was the last one to climb out. Once he had crawled up the rungs, one by one, the faithful

mastiff ran over to his master and started to lovingly lick mulch and leaves off his face.

"Stop it, William!" snorted the boy whose dignity had already been trampled more than enough. He ignored Minerva, and feeling his way, headed with

his friends towards the beach where they had left their boat.

The others followed them. “Don’t play any tricks now,” Ravi warned them. “Our pockets are full of poisonous millipedes.”

“Don’t worry if you can’t see right yet,” Henrietta said when the whole gang was on board. “The current will push you towards the port.”

“So long, Gilbert!” Minerva waved, while thc little boat pulled away from the shore. “I’m so sorry, but it looks like we’ve won this time too!”

The four friends raised their arms in the air, celebrating.

“We made it!” Ravi yelled.

“Minerva, you are a real genius,” Thomasina said, putting her arms around her.

“You’re a hero!” Henrietta cried, joining the hug.

The girl blushed and wrinkled her freckled nose. “Oh, it’s all thanks to the people who drew the map,” she replied, though she was over the moon.

Their excitement, however, was far from over...

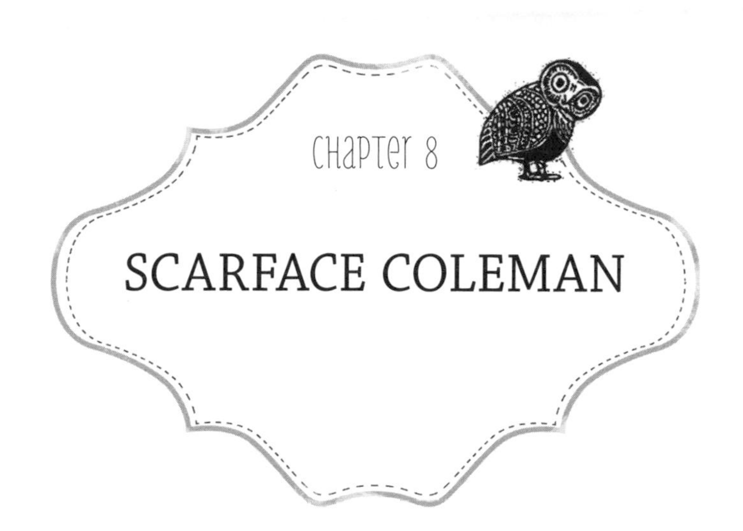

Chapter 8

SCARFACE COLEMAN

Ding! Ding! Ding! Bells rang out among the trees behind them.

"The alarm!" Ravi shouted. "Someone's by the nests right now!"

Fortunately, it was just Timothy. Hiding behind a bush, Minerva and the others watched him.

The innkeeper checked the nests, making sure they were all still intact. He measured the sand temperature, scratched his chin, and then left, muttering about having things to do for the village festival.

The moment that his boat was far enough from the shore, four heads popped up from the bush.

"He almost caught us." Ravi sighed.

"We were lucky," Minerva agreed. "Timothy was in such a hurry that he didn't notice our footprints in the sand. We forgot to rub them out."

They were about to leave their hideout, when Henrietta stopped them. "There's someone there!"

They stepped back in the nick of time. Someone had been hiding in a boat behind some rocks, waiting for Timothy to leave. A man climbed off the boat into the water and pulled it ashore.

"Look! That's Coleman!" Minerva whispered. "He followed Timothy unnoticed."

Four pairs of eyes hidden behind leaves watched the man's every move.

Now that he could see his face clearly, Ravi noticed that a long scar ran across his right cheek, just like the pirate in his nightmare. He was tall and beefy and had a potbelly. Getting the better of him was not going to be easy at all.

Coleman unloaded a spade and four wicker baskets from his boat. He looked at the little sand dunes and licked his lips, like a man about to stuff his face. "Here I come, my dear golden eggs!" he exclaimed. "Thanks to you, I'll make buckets of money."

Then he grabbed the spade and made for the nearest nest.

The bush rustled.

"We have to stop him!" whispered Ravi.

"But how?" Henrietta replied.

"We haven't had time to reset the traps," Thomasina reminded them.

They were helpless against Coleman, but something had to be done or else the turtles were history.

Minerva made a split-second decision. *"Chaaarge!"* she yelled, suddenly emerging from behind the bush and darting towards the man.

Coleman was so startled he dropped the spade.

"What on earth..." he mumbled. He promptly regained his composure, though, and ran after Minerva who, in the meantime, had turned around

and began running away from him. “Hey, you! Come here straight away!” he yelled at her. “Stop!”

The moment he walked past the bush, three pairs of arms reached for his feet and made him stumble and fall face first into the sand. “I’ll be darned!” the crook cried. “Who are you?” he shouted, seeing the children. “What are you doing here?”

In answer to that question, the children dashed in the same direction Minerva had gone, but the man managed to grab Henrietta’s ankle.

“Gotcha!” he shouted. He got to his feet and tried to hold the little girl still: she was as slippery as an eel. “Hey, I’m talking to you out there!” he yelled at the trees. “Unless you want something to happen to your friend, I suggest you all come back here!”

They had no choice: all three of them came back and frowned at the villain.

“Let her go!” Ravi said.

Coleman leered. “Not yet, boy. There’s a time for everything. Are you all here?” he asked, glancing around.

"It's just the four of us," Minerva answered. "Now, let our friend go!"

The man shook his head. "Do as I say, and nothing will happen to you. Now, be good children and go sit around that log down there." Dragging Henrietta, Coleman walked to the boat and came back with a long piece of rope and four shorter pieces. "Tie your hands behind your backs. Help each other if you need to," he ordered. "And don't you even think about cheating!" Finally, he put the Henrietta next to the others and tied them all to the log.

"I don't want to hurt you," he reassured them. "I'll just take my eggs and leave. Then I'll send somebody over to rescue you. I'll tell them I saw some children all by themselves on the island. By the time they find you, I'll be far away with my loot. There," he concluded, making sure that the rope was tight enough. "I don't wanna hear a pin drop," he warned them. "I have very important work to do." He turned his back on the children and went to recover his spade.

Ravi looked at Minerva, who was sitting right

next to him. Her eyes were aflame with her ancestor's fighting spirit.

"I tried to tie a loose knot in yours," he whispered in her ear. "See if you can free yourself."

Minerva moved her fingers. "I think I can do it," she whispered. She struggled but finally managed to yank her hands free of the rope. She glanced at Coleman. Thankfully, he still had his back to them. With a lightning movement, she brought the tiny flute she always kept around her neck to her mouth and whistled: *TOOT! TOOT!*

The man turned with a jerk. "What?!"

When he realized that Minerva had freed her hands, he walked towards her with a threatening look in his eyes. “Children, I’m tired of your games. If you don’t stay put and quiet I’ll–”

He couldn’t finish his sentence, though, because at that precise moment the sky turned black, and the air was filled with high-pitched shrills and the fluttering of wings.

The man looked up and turned pale. Dozens of snow white owls were nosediving him at high speeds. And there were seagulls, cormorants, carrion crows, and, though in smaller numbers, even hawks and eagles. At the head of the flock, as if leading the attack, was little Napoleon. “Smelly onion!” he shrieked with his shrill voice. “Hairy beet!”

“Hooray! Here comes the air defence!” Ravi cheered.

“Go get him, Napoleon!” Thomasina yelled.

“Show him!” Henrietta spurred him on.

“Help!” squealed Coleman, whirling his arms to keep the attackers away.

His efforts were totally in vain, though: the owls and their allies kept attacking relentlessly.

"Dirty maggot!" Napoleon croaked. "Snail slime!"

Scared out of his wits, the man ran towards the sea, trying to cover his head with his hands. With great effort, he managed to push his boat into the water, leaving behind his spade and baskets, and started out, rowing like a madman.

Minerva untied her friends' wrists as fast as she could. As soon as they were all free of the ropes, they rushed to the shore. They saw Coleman's boat speeding towards the port as if he'd turned on its turbo boost, a huge flock of birds hot on his heels.

"Hooray!" Thomasina yelled, doing a wild victory dance with Henrietta and Ravi. "We did it!"

They were all so happy that it took them a while to realize that Minerva was not taking part in their celebration.

Their red-haired friend was sitting on the sand with a dismayed look on her face, staring at something she held in her hand.

"What happened?" asked Ravi, walking up to her.

The girl showed him her flute. "It fell and … it broke."

Thomasina crouched in front of her. "Oh, I'm sorry … I'm sure we can fix it, though!" She delicately picked up the pieces and studied them. "Look, it's not really broken at all."

The flute had come apart along its length, and the two sections fit back together perfectly.

Thomasina put it back together with a *click* and gave it to her friend.

"Oh, I was so scared." Minerva sighed. She opened the flute, closed it, opened it again, and looked inside it. "Hey! There's something written here!"

They all closed in to take a better look. Inside the flute there was an inscription made with a thin point.

"This is for you, my dear girl, may you be forever safe," Thomasina read aloud. *"The owls will be your guardians."*

There was also a tiny owl with the words *Domina Noctuae* written around it.

"The Lady of the Owls," Minerva translated. Then, she opened her green eyes wide. "Oh my gosh, that means..." In her excitement, she sprang to her feet and started waving the flute. "This is the amulet that Althea left to her daughter to protect her ... just like it says in the letter we found in the City of the Ravagers! Look: the symbol of the owl looks exactly

the same as the one we found on the wax seal next to her signature."

The discovery left them speechless for a moment. It was an amazing discovery: the flute hidden inside the wall in Lizard Manor was Althea's amulet!

Minerva stared at the small instrument in awe. She had kept it around her neck all that time, totally unaware that it had once belonged to her mysterious and fascinating ancestor. She squeezed it and suddenly felt closer to her, closer to the Lady of the Owls who had outwitted everybody and had managed to put her hands on an invaluable treasure!

Thomasina shook her out of her thoughts by clapping her hands. "So how about celebrating our victory?"

"Good idea, baby!" croaked Napoleon who had just come back from his victorious mission.

With an air of self-importance, the small parrot perched on Thomasina's shoulder. And for the first time since they had met him, the children thought the bird was smiling.

Chapter 9

THE HIDDEN TREASURE

Later that day, the gang celebrated by eating grilled fish and strawberry jam near the nests.

They sat together in a spot where they could keep an eye on the little sand dunes and be able to admire the sunset at the same time. The sun was red like a ripe raspberry, and it was diving into the water.

The sky was mottled with a thousand shades of orange, purple and candyfloss pink, while a light, sweet-scented sea breeze blew the flag that read "Free Republic of the Turtles". They had brought it to the beach as a sign of victory.

"Ow!" groaned Ravi, holding his full belly in his hands. As he often did when he overate, he let out a loud belch, spoiling the romantic sunset. "Excuse me," he muttered, bringing a hand to his mouth.

"You lousy pig!" croaked Napoleon, taking off in flight and vanishing from sight in the inner part of the island.

Henrietta and Thomasina burst out laughing, and Ravi, once he had overcome his initial feeling of embarrassment, joined the two girls.

I'm a rude sea dog now, he thought, relaxing. He could finally savour the triumphs of that day without worrying: not only had they managed to protect the turtles, but they had also made an extremely important discovery regarding Minerva's story.

The boy turned towards her and saw that she had a serious look on her face. "Are you okay?" he asked.

Minerva smiled at him. Feeling the weight of the tiny flute gave her a renewed sense of safety. "Yes … I was just thinking about all the things we still have to discover," she answered.

"The Ravagers' treasure, for instance!" Thomasina immediately butted in.

"First of all, however, we have to find out what happened to Althea's daughter," Ravi pointed out. "Whether she managed to find the treasure and what she did with it..."

Henrietta was looking at them with a pinch of envy. "I'll be so sad when I have to leave Pembrose." She sighed. "I won't know anything about your adventures anymore."

The others were saddened by that thought too: by now they considered Henrietta a full member of their secret club.

"We'll stay in touch!" Thomasina insisted. "Better still, why don't you move to Cornwall?" she said. "We have a very good school in Pembrose, you know?"

"And in Lizard Manor, we have a huge library crammed with books about just everything you can think of," Minerva said, trying to tempt her.

"And my mum makes delicious snacks," Ravi added. "Genuine Indian treats!"

"Besides, you can't leave without seeing our hide-out in the moor," Thomasina added. "You're going to love it: we've filled it with everything you need to go on adventures!"

When she met Ravi's, Minerva's and Thomasina's eyes, Henrietta felt a lump in her throat as she shook her head. "I'm sorry, but I really can't stay in Cornwall."

"Is it because of your secret?" Ravi asked.

Henrietta hesitated, then said, "Well ... in part."

"Can't you tell us what it's about yet?" Thomasina asked.

Hesitation flickered in the girl's dark eyes. "No, I'm sorry. But I will tell you all before I leave," she promised.

The thought of Henrietta's departure dampened their enthusiasm a bit. Fortunately, though, nature itself diverted their attention: something magical was happening on the beach.

"Look!" cried Ravi, the first to realize what was going on.

A tiny turtle was crawling out of a sand dune. First came the little head, then the light blue shell, and finally the tiny tail. Stunned by the new freedom, the creature started shaking its miniature flippers, but it did not move at all. It didn't give up, though, and kept trying until it conquered a few centimetres. Animated by that victory, the turtle seemed to gain confidence and coordination. Another little head popped up behind it, then another and another still…

Minerva exclaimed, "There's so many of them!"

The young blue turtles started moving left and right, choosing no particular direction.

Ravi was itching to give them a little push. "Are you really sure we're not supposed to help them?" he begged Thomasina.

She shook her head. "No. The book says that any contact with humans could make them lose their sense of orientation forever." The girl looked over at the sea. It was almost dark, but the faint and shaky light of the stars reflected on the water. "Actually, there is something else that we can do."

She fetched the torch from her bag. "We can help them find the sea."

Wasting no time, she stood up and pointed the torch towards the water: the turtles moved in that direction. Thomasina pointed the beam forwards and the little ones kept following it.

"It works!" Ravi cheered. He was so awestruck by Thomasina's intelligence that he threw his arms around her without thinking. Then he let her go and stepped back, red like a tomato, and stuttered, "Well, yeah, you know ... that's a really clever idea."

Thomasina smiled at him and moved the light a bit further: the small sea creatures followed it, making a huge effort to crawl across the sand using their flippers. Finally, they reached the water's edge, where for the first time in their short life, they were caressed by the sea water.

The children, who had carefully and quietly followed their every moves, held their breaths.

The little turtles were struggling against the waves that kept pushing them back to shore.

"There's nothing else we can do to help them now," Thomasina whispered, lowering the torch.

Ravi clenched his fists to resist the urge to intervene. To him, it looked like an impossible challenge: the fight between the great Atlantic Ocean and a turtle the size of a peanut. "C'mon, little ones!" he encouraged them. "Come on! You can do it!"

The tiny creatures were washed back ashore by the undertow, but they didn't give up: they moved forwards on the water's edge and were pushed back once again, and again, until ... they all disappeared in the water.

"They made it!" shouted an amazed Minerva.

It was such an extraordinary event that the four children simply stood scanning the sea, almost expecting to suddenly see the turtles swimming back to shore. However, they never came back. Their journey towards unknown and faraway places had begun.

The gang hugged and started hopping joyfully.

"Hooray!" Ravi cheered. He was very proud of his little turtles.

"Hey, look! There's more on the way!" exclaimed Henrietta, gesturing towards a sand dune that was teeming with tiny turtles.

Thomasina promptly flashed a light towards the water to guide the new hatchlings.

As the eggs hatched, the children helped the little creatures to the water. When the last one had vanished into the sea, they flopped down on the sand and fell asleep. It had been a long and amazing night.

The snowy owl that flew over from the mainland found them like that: lying next to one another under the heavenly vault dotted with stars, a huge smile fixed on their faces.

The grand creature of the night perched on a branch and rolled his round yellow eyes. *"Woot! Woot!"* he hooted, moving his feathery head.

He would watch over them until daybreak.

* * *

Minerva was awakened by a ray of light dancing on her eyelids. At first she didn't know where she

was, but then she heard the waves crashing on the shore and the memory of the previous night came back to her immediately. She sat up, stretched and glanced about: the sand was full of tiny tracks.

"Woot! Woot!" went the snowy owl perched on the branch over her head.

Minerva looked up. "Good morning, Augustus!" she said. "Thanks for helping us yesterday."

The majestic creature rolled his yellow eyes and took off, gracefully flapping his snow white wings. *"Woot! Woot!"* he hooted, soaring higher and higher.

"Don't worry," Minerva said, waving goodbye. "We're coming back home today!"

"What's happening?" asked Ravi, rubbing his eyes. "Who's talking?"

The other two girls woke up too.

"I am so tired…" Thomasina mumbled.

"What time is it?" Henrietta asked, yawning.

Thomasina checked an alarm clock that she carried in her bag. "Nine o'clock on the dot."

"Oh no! We slept too long!" Henrietta panicked.

"We must get back to Pembrose. The scouts' bus will be back in an hour!"

The children rushed to the fort to pick up their bags and camping gear.

Minerva was putting the leftover strawberry jam into her rucksack when a jar rolled against the wall of the fort. As she bent down to pick it up, she noticed something strange. "Hey, come and take a look at this!" she said.

Her friends walked over to where she was and saw that Minerva was studying a rock at the base of the wall: it jutted out somewhat more than the others, as if it could be pulled out. The red-haired girl grabbed it firmly with two hands and pulled. With a great effort, she managed to yank it out. The stone was hollow like a drawer, and there was a roll of coarse cloth inside.

Minerva took it and opened it, revealing a yellowed rolled piece of paper. Once she had finished studying it, her jaw dropped. "Listen to what it says. *In this year of the Lord 1750*," she began to read,

"His Majesty George II, by hand of the excellent district governor Edmund de Waall, presents Timothy Long, owner of the Fishbone Inn, located in the town of Pembrose, Cornwall, with Turtle Island, so that he may benefit from it for the rest of his life and then pass it on to his descendants..." Minerva stopped reading. "Do you think this Timothy Long is an ancestor of our Timothy?"

"He must be," Thomasina said. "They have the same name. And my father told me that the Fishbone Inn is very old."

Minerva pointed her finger at the bottom of the page. "Here is the king's signature ... *George II of England*," she read.

Underneath there was a wax seal engraved with a crown in the middle of a lion and a unicorn. Every subject of Great Britain, regardless if child or grown-up, knew that those were the symbols of royalty.

"Wow!" Thomasina said. "It means that it's a genuine royal document."

Ravi clapped his hands. "This means that ... Turtle Island belongs to Timothy!"

"And from now on no one will be allowed to come here without his permission," Henrietta concluded.

Minerva smiled. "The turtles will be safe forever!"

"I wonder if Timothy will let us watch the hatching every now and then," Ravi said with a sigh.

Henrietta started. "Come on, there's no time to waste. We have to go *right now*!"

Minerva rolled up the page. "We'll give this to Timothy as soon as we get back to Pembrose," she said, slipping it into her pocket.

Then they darted down to the beach, carrying their bags. They pushed the *Althea* out of its hiding place under the bushes and pulled it into the water. They put all their belongings in the boat and put on their life jackets.

Napoleon arrived just in time. He perched on Minerva's shoulder and squawked, "Full speed ahead!"

"Hey! I'm the captain!" Ravi blurted out.

"Landlubber!" Napoleon croaked.

Ravi burst into laughter. "This is a mutiny!" Then he dipped the oars, and the boat went out into the open water, headed for Pembrose.

They all turned back to look at the island and waved goodbye, like you would do with a dear friend.

Minerva felt a touch of sadness: she would never forget the night the baby turtles had reached the sea and the adventures they had lived together. She put a hand on her heart, where her tiny flute was. Luckily, there were still many mysteries to solve and many adventures ahead of them!

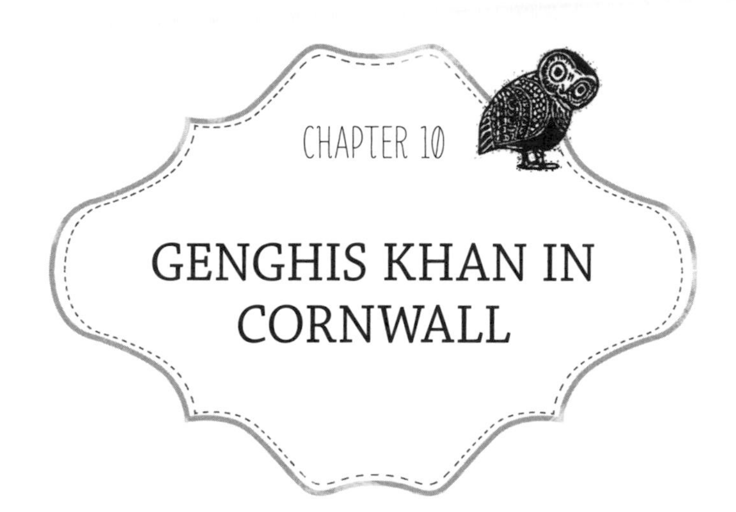

CHAPTER 10

GENGHIS KHAN IN CORNWALL

By the time the *Althea* docked, the last preparations for the Seaman's Fest were in full swing. The white, red and blue flags of the Royal Navy fluttered outside the windows of cottages, and streets were crowded with tourists and well-dressed villagers. At the wharf, everything was ready to start frying huge quantities of fish and chips, which would then be handed out wrapped in newspaper. Standing on a makeshift stage, the Pembrose choir and marching band were rehearsing "Foam, Waves and Billows!"

The children tied up the boat in a hidden spot at the end of the dock and got off, unloading their rucksacks and suitcases. They took off the life jackets and left them in the boat with the rest of their gear.

Then they looked at each other with hesitation. It was time to say goodbye, but Ravi, Minerva and Thomasina didn't look too excited at that idea.

"You must rush back to the main square," Henrietta urged them. "The scouts' bus will be there any minute. Your parents and Mrs Flopps are going to be there, waiting for you. If they don't see you, you might get caught."

"What are you going to do?" Minerva asked.

"Unfortunately, my holiday in Pembrose is over," Henrietta said with a sigh. "Now I have to run and pack. But come say goodbye here at eight, when the party starts."

"Are you going to tell us your secret then?" asked Ravi, somewhat relieved by the possibility.

Henrietta smiled. "Yes, I always keep my promises." She winked at him. Then she put on her sailor

hat and pulled it over her forehead almost over her eyes, turning once again into the cocky and somewhat cheeky boy they had met just a few days before. "See you later! Don't be late," she said with a wily smile, "or you'll never know my secret!" She took off, but before she disappeared around a corner, she stopped and turned to wave them goodbye.

The three friends sighed; their adventure was really over now.

Ravi glanced around. "Now's the time to go," he whispered. "No one will see us in all that commotion."

They stole along Plum Tree Avenue, until Minerva suddenly stopped.

"Quick, hide!" she whispered.

They all took shelter behind a basket full of apples and craned their neck to take a look.

Timothy had just finished loading three suitcases on Lola's cart. "Mr Coleman!" he said. "It's all ready."

An instant later, the man walked out of the inn's main door. He was very different from the last time they had seen him: he looked as white as a ghost

and seemed shy and wary. He kept glancing around nervously, but mostly, he kept looking up, as if he were afraid that something might fall on his head. He climbed on the cart next to Timothy and said, “Let’s hurry … I-I mean,” he stammered. “I have a very important meeting in London.”

“Did you hear that?” Timothy asked the quiet mare. “Giddy up, Lola!”

The peaceful, hazel-eyed horse neighed and moved with its usual slowness, just like a noble-woman on a relaxing stroll.

Coleman snorted. “I said I’m in a hurry!”

It was then that Napoleon flew off Minerva’s shoulder. “Rogue ahead!” he croaked. “Let the scoun-drel have it!”

The effect on Coleman was devastating: he turned as green as a bell pepper and grabbed his suitcase to cover his head.

The innkeeper smiled at him. “Don’t be afraid of Napoleon, Mr Coleman. He’s just a little parrot.”

But the man kept the suitcase over his head.

"I felt a raindrop," he mumbled. "And I don't have my umbrella. Couldn't your horse go a little bit faster?"

Hidden behind the basket, the three children managed to stifle their laughter until Lola was far enough away. Then they rolled around on the ground, holding their bellies.

"Ha-ha! That was priceless!" Ravi cried.

"Serves him right!" Thomasina said, crying with laughter. "He got what he deserved."

"Yes, I think he's learnt his lesson," Minerva said. Then she fished the title deed to Turtle Island out of her pocket and slipped it into the restaurant's mailbox. She turned and looked at her friends. "Remember, no one has to know that we had a hand in this," she said seriously. "Not even Timothy."

Ravi and Thomasina nodded gravely. When they had founded the Order of the Owls, they had taken an oath: they would always be the nameless defenders of Pembrose.

When they got to the church, the scouts' bus had just pulled in, so Minerva, Ravi and Thomasina could easily mingle with the crowd of children that were pouring out into the square.

"See you later!" Minerva whispered as they went their separate ways. "Remember, mouths zipped!"

* * *

That evening, they all met in the square by the little church. The village glowed with the light of many small lanterns propped on the windowsills,

and the tempting smell of deep-fried foods was already hanging in the air.

"Mmm," Ravi said, sniffing the air. "I feel like eating at least a tonne of chips! And a lot of fish too!"

"You're always thinking about your stomach," Thomasina said with disapproval, smoothing her baby pink skirt.

"What's wrong with that?" Ravi protested. "We practically starved while wc were on the island! Anyway ... um," he muttered to make it up to her. "You look great in pink."

Thomasina twirled. "Really? Do you think so?"

"I do. And Minerva looks great too," Ravi added.

His friend smiled. She was wearing an outfit she had found in a wardrobe in one of Lizard Manor's many rooms. It was a sailor suit – red, white and blue: the colours of the Union Jack. "I bet this uniform belonged to one of my ancestors who must have been a captain," she guessed.

At that precise moment, the church bell struck eight.

"We have to get to the harbour right now!" Ravi urged. "Come on, before we miss Henrietta."

They hurried down to the wharf and looked around, a bit anxious. It was bustling with couples walking arm in arm, elderly ladies scoffing up fish and chips, and brawny, tattooed sailors.

"I wonder if Henrietta is really going to come," Ravi whispered, somewhat disappointed that she was not already there waiting for them.

"She promised she would," Minerva reminded him.

"I'm sure she'll show up soon," Thomasina said.

And so they stood there in the midst of tourists and villagers, and still there was no sign of Henrietta.

"Hello, don't you recognize me?" a joyful voice asked from behind them.

They all turned around, and their jaws dropped.

"But ... but ... w-what?" Ravi stammered.

Henrietta didn't look like herself anymore. And she didn't look like Henry either. She had become a totally different person.

"Wow!" cried Minerva.

"Oh, what a beautiful dress!" Thomasina said with a hint of envy.

"Surprise!" Henrietta said.

The three children kept staring at her with their eyes wide open.

The girl's smooth hair hung around her shoulders. She was wearing a two-piece outfit: loose sky-blue harem trousers and a jacket of the same colour with golden trimming and long puffball sleeves. Her feet were clad in fancy sandals decorated with beads. She looked like a character from Arabian Nights.

"This is a traditional outfit from my country," she explained.

"What coun..." Ravi began to ask. However, he saw something even more amazing, which froze the words in his mouth.

An imposing figure had just stepped next to Henrietta with a protective attitude. It was a gigantic Asian man with a Genghis Kahn-like moustache that drooped down to his chin, jet-black hair tied into a

long ponytail, and a serious expression on his face. He was wearing a flashy yellow tunic suit and trousers with red dragon embroidery and matching slippers.

While the gang stared at him awestruck, the man joined his hands and gave a bow.

"This is Wang," Henrietta said.

Minerva returned the bow, and then so did the other two.

"Pleased to meet you, Mr Wang," they all said.

But that was not the last extraordinary sight of the evening.

Ravi was the first to see it out of the corner of his eye. "Look at that!" he exclaimed, pointing to the sea.

A three-mast ship had just rounded Cape Pembrose with its sails unfurled and puffed out by the wind. A great red flag with a golden crown fluttered in the wind atop the mainmast.

Two figures were visible on the bridge, but they were too far away to make out the faces. Henrietta seemed to know who they were, because she started waving to them. Then she turned towards her friends. "Those are my parents," she said through a wide smile. "I haven't seen them in months..."

Unable to help himself, Ravi finally blurted out, "Come on now! Won't you tell us who you are?"

Henrietta burst out laughing. "You're right, Ravi. A promise is a promise."

Minerva was in awe of the sailing ship. "Are your parents a king and a queen?" she asked, pointing at the flag cracking in the wind.

Her friend nodded. "Yes, they are," she confirmed.

"My dad is the king of a small state on the Arabian Sea. My mum's English, and she's the one who chose my name, Henrietta. I am attending a special music school in England – a very exclusive school where everybody's very serious and treats me like 'Her Highness' all the time. My parents are so busy running our country that I only see them during the winter holidays and for a couple of days in the summer." She sighed. "I couldn't reveal my identity before because I had promised them I wouldn't. Actually, my parents are always very concerned about my safety. That's why Wang is here," she added, pointing at the enormous man.

He gave another bow, but his face remained expressionless.

"You mean he's your bodyguard?" whispered a slightly intimidated Ravi.

"Something like that," Henrietta replied. "He's like a second father to me. I've known him since I was born, and he taught me everything I know about the sea. Wang comes from Canton and was a sailor before

my parents took him on. He's had a lot of adventures in the Indian Ocean. He used to tell me stories when I was a child to help me sleep. That's why I became so interested in having my own adventures," she said with a sigh. "Sometimes I'm so tired of living the life of a princess, you know, I wish I were someone else..."

"Is that the reason why you dressed up as a boy?" Minerva inquired.

Henrietta smiled. "Yes. I made a deal with Wang," she explained. "A few days of the year he gives me permission to live a different life. This year I decided I would be a cabin boy, and I would look at the world through my binoculars." She grinned. "Then I met you and immediately knew you were special."

"So you spied on us, didn't you?" Ravi butted in.

"I did, at first ... then I just wanted to be your friend."

"What do your parents think?" Thomasina asked. "Do they know what you do during the summer?"

Henrietta took on a rather guilty look. "Actually,

they know nothing about it. It's a secret between Wang and me. He just can't say no to me. He's been like that since I was a little girl." She smiled, giving a look full of love to her protector. "He's always watching over me, though. This time, however, I managed to get away from him too! So I experienced a real adventure on my own with you all ... and it's been a fantastic experience! I don't know how to thank you all!"

"Where are you going to go now?" Minerva asked.

"Wang picked me up at school and brought me here to Pembrose to wait for my parents. They have rented a house out of town. From here we're going to sail to Ireland, where we're going to spend a few days all together."

The gang turned to face the sea. The huge sailing ship had almost entered the harbour, and they could now see the name on the side of the hull, *Shangri-la*, and the faces of the man and the woman standing on the bridge. They were waving their hands.

Henrietta's face lit up. "I can't wait to hug them!"

She sighed. "Like I said, I spend very little time with them. They're always busy and I'm always at school."

"Well, now you'll spend time together on that luxurious three-mast," said Ravi with a hint of envy. The role of captain had started to grow on him and a rowing boat was nothing like a sailing ship.

"But I already miss our little boat!" said Henrietta, as if she had read his mind. "You know, I've never met anyone like you three and I hope that, you know..." She blushed. "I hope I can come back here next year if ... you know ... you'll have me."

In answer to that question, Minerva hugged her, and Ravi and Thomasina immediately followed.

"Oh," she said, "I'm going to miss you so much!"

In the meantime, the ship had reached the pier. "Henrietta!" a woman's voice called.

"It's Mum," said the girl, letting go of her friends. She wiped a teardrop off her face. "I really have to go now." She smiled. "I'll see you next year!"

Escorted by the unflinching and monumental Wang, she made for the *Shangri-la*.

Halfway through the gangway, she turned to look at her friends for the last time.

"Bye, Henrietta!" Ravi shouted. "Don't forget us!"

"We're going to miss you too so much!" Thomasina yelled.

"You're part of the Order of the Owls now!" added Minerva.

Henrietta smiled, then she turned around and ran into her parents' open arms.

When she saw that, Minerva's heart sank just a little. She grabbed the flute with both hands and felt Ravi and Thomasina step closer to her – as protective as the gigantic Wang.

As they watched the ship leave the pier and glide elegantly into the open water, the crack of the first fireworks echoed in the air. Red, green, yellow and blue dazzling flowers exploded in the sky and then plunged into the water like shooting stars. The *Shangri-la* was now floating in a sea like no one had ever seen in Cornwall – one alight with colours.

The orchestra and the Happy Fisherman Choir

performed "Let Us Sail Away to the Sea". It was the night's highlight, and everybody on the wharf started dancing.

Even Timothy was hopping around enthusiastically, hugging Gwendolyn. "Something incredible has happened!" he cried as he twirled past them. "Even though ... you see ... it's still a secret," he added.

The three friends exchanged a look.

"Don't say anything then!" Minerva said.

"But we are very happy for you," added Ravi, winking at him.

The children walked away giggling and headed to the boat to gather the rest of their gear.

The *Althea* was tied to the post at the end of the pier, exactly where they had left it. Something was different, though: there was an envelope on top of the pile of life jackets.

Ravi picked it up. "It's for Minerva," he said after reading the address.

"It must be another letter from the Dragon!" an excited Thomasina exclaimed.

They looked around. All the inhabitants of Pembrose were on the wharf: Timothy, Oliver, the Bartholomew sisters, Agatha, Dr Gerald, Ravi's mother, Father Mullet, fishermen and old ladies of the charity club. Could the Dragon be one of them?

"What are you waiting for? Open it!" snapped Thomasina impatiently.

Minerva tore the envelope open and slipped out a piece of paper. She skimmed it, frowning. "Signed by the Dragon," she confirmed.

"What does it say?" Ravi asked.

"Yeah, why don't you read it?" Thomasina snorted.

The crumples on Minerva's forehead eased up. "Everyone," she said with a big smile, "I think we're in for many more adventures soon. Listen to this: *On Turtle Island you have been. / And to your safety the owls have seen / luck won't always be there, though.../ so don't you say I didn't let you know!"* she read. *"Your dear friend, the Dragon."*

ELISA PURICELLI GUERRA

Elisa at the age of 3

As a child, I had red hair. It was so red that it led to several nicknames, the prettiest of which was Carrot. With my red hair, I wanted to be Pippi Longstocking for two reasons. The first reason was that I wanted to have the strength to lift a horse and show him to everyone! The second was that every night my mother read Astrid Lindgren's books to me until she nearly lost her voice (or until I graciously allowed her to go to bed). As I fell asleep each night, I hoped to wake up at Villa Villacolle. Instead, I found myself in Milan. What a great disappointment!

After all of Lindgren's books were read and reread, my mother, with the excuse that I was grown up, refused to continue to read them again. So I began to tell stories myself. They were serialized stories, each more and more intricate than the one before and chock-full of interesting characters. Pity then, the next morning, when I would always forget everything.

Elisa today

At that point I had no choice; I started to read myself. I still remember the book that I chose: a giant-sized edition of the Brothers Grimm fairy tales with a blue cloth cover.

Today my hair is less red, but reading is still my favourite pastime. It's a shame it's not a profession because it would be perfect for me!

GABO LEÓN BERNSTEIN

I was born in Buenos Aires, Argentina, and have had to overcome many obstacles to become an illustrator.

"You cannot draw there," my mum said to me, pointing to the wall that was smeared.

"You cannot draw there," the teacher said to me, pointing to the school book that was messed up.

"Draw where you want to ... but you were supposed to hand over the pictures last week," my publishers say to me, pointing to the calendar.

Currently I illustrate children's books, and I'm interested in video games and animation projects. The more I try to learn to play the violin, the more I am convinced that illustrating is my life and my passion. My cat and the neighbours rejoice in it.

Gabo

YOU CAN FIND
MORE
GREAT
BOOKS
FROM
RAINTREE AT
WWW.RAINTREE.CO.U